The Body in the Butter Churn

a Green Mountain whodunit

Elaine Magalis (signature)

Elaine Magalis

This is a work of fiction. All characters and events portrayed in this book are fictitious and not intended to represent real people or places.

Although the locale where this story takes place is a real one, various liberties have been taken, and this book does not purport to offer an exact depiction of any particular place or location.

To the Old Stone House
and all who have loved her

CONTENTS

Acknowledgments

Thanks to those who have read this book in manuscript, and made suggestions and corrections, especially Pam Crandall, Maureen James, Paula Behnken, Tracy Martin and Joan Graul. Special thanks to Jeannine Young who assiduously proofread it!

Preface

Years ago, I worked as the education director at a museum much like the one in this book. No murder ever took place there so far as I know; in fact, not even a crime of any note. Nevertheless, the kids I worked with knew the place was not quite right: they caught sight of ghosts walking the hallways; they knew the past was more alive there than the present. They wanted a murder, or at least something made for television, to happen. This book is one small way to redress what I could never deliver.

The museum is the real star and central player in this book. Some of the other characters are based on complicated combinations of people who have lived and worked there, served up with a large measure of imagination. But the museum is pretty much the character it's always been.

The Body in the
Butter Churn

I

The death of Old Aggie

It was a cool autumn morning, the best time to fish in the farm pond across the road, but Alex Churchill was stuck in the Old Shrubsbury School House Museum with a bunch of mind-numbing grown-ups, and he was getting impatient. He'd promised Ms. Mulholland to help shine up some nineteenth century windows before he went fishing, and fishing in this particular water hole was much better earlier than later. Everyone was waiting for Agatha Hamilton to appear and tell them something "of great import." To give the grown-ups in the company credit, none of them wanted to be here any more than Alex, except that the old woman had hinted that she had something to say about her fortune and the future of the museum. When Mrs. Hamilton called, they all scrambled, even though, as director Adrian Dabney had been known to mutter, she was just the wealthy busybody who lived across the road.

No one liked Agatha Hamilton. The kids who hung out at

the museum called her "Old Aggie" behind her back. Even Alex, who was well-behaved to a fault, once ticked her off so badly she chased him with a butter paddle, screeching the whole time like a banshee—eeiiyyeee, eeiiyyeee.

"Just like her to waste our time this way," complained Principal Plumbwell, who was late for an appointment at Shrubsbury Elementary School. "I don't understand why she's always so rude," murmured Major Shelton's wife who was easily insulted. "Same old, same old," said Adrian Dabney. "We'll give her a few more minutes. And then, it's off and out of here." He twinkled at them, one by one. "Perhaps, we could pass the time with some edifying historical tidbit. Maybe something from the kitchen since that happens to be where we are. Lori, any ideas?"

Lori looked flustered, as if he'd asked her something recondite, unfathomable. "I don't know. I'm just not inspired this morning. Although, the kitchen is the most inspiring room in the museum and if I had any ideas—"

"Perhaps we could ask Ms. Mulholland to tell us about the root cellar. It's behind that door," Adrian said—smiling at the board members who might not know—and pointing. "Or perhaps she could show us how the Star butter churn works." He gave the churn a sharp tap.

"Oh, please. Let's do the butter churn." said Lori, suddenly eager. "It's much more interesting than that silly cellar. And I've always wondered how to make butter with it."

"Why it's not difficult at all, Lori," said Ms. Mulholland.

"I thought you knew. It's like any other butter churn, just bigger and without the paddles inside that some churns have. Instead you turn the crank and the barrel tumbles end over end until the butter is formed."

She started to turn the crank handle to spin the barrel, but it didn't budge.

"This is much larger than most churns, even Star churns, although there are some that are even bigger. The larger the barrel, the fewer revolutions a minute need to be cranked."

She pulled, she pushed and still, it stuck. Alex joined her and they struggled with it together. When the barrel finally did move, just a bit, something clunked inside.

"Probably," said Ms. Mulholland brightly, "the high school students are playing a joke on us. They've done this before—filled the churn with tennis shoes and rocks. Help me open the cover, Alex."

They struggled together again, this time to open the cover. "One disadvantage of this kind of churn is that it needs to be sealed tight so it won't leak."

When they finally managed to pry the cover from the top, there was something inside—cloth, a loose shoe… Tasha Mulholland reached in and then stopped, her eyes wide, a small hoarse sound coming from her throat. Alex dropped the cover. Clunk. It rolled across the floor. Old Aggie was in the churn staring at them. She'd been crammed in, bottom first. As small as she was, she was a tight fit. Wrinkled and gray like crumpled up newspaper, covered with sticky blood like she'd rusted, she'd been slashed across the throat.

Ms. Mulholland stood flat-footed in front of the churn, as if Aggie were naked instead of dead and needed to be shielded from everyone's inquisitive eyes. "I'm sorry," she murmured in a low, raspy voice. "It looks like Aggie's in the butter churn, and dead. Not even wearing her butter-making apron. Just dead."

When Alex's mother saw the dead woman staring at them, wild-eyed, accusing, she grabbed Alex and smothered him to her in a hug so big he couldn't look anymore. By the time he wriggled away he was so embarrassed he'd almost forgotten his first horror at the murder, but what could he do? She didn't expect life to be like TV and if it was, she expected to be able to block it.

By the time the police and the coroner got to the museum, rigor mortis had set in and it was almost impossible to get Aggie out. So they took the churn away too.

It was weird for there to be a murder in Shrubsbury, Vermont, because the town was a bore, but Alex supposed that if it was going to happen at all, the Old Shrubsbury School House was the perfect place for it. Standing higher than the houses, higher than the church steeple, higher even than the old trees that fronted it, unexpected, lonely somehow on the plateau that was the village, light danced in its forty-eight windows on bright summer days, but shadows skulked through the building the rest of the time. Even though he'd spent most of the summer working there, when he least expected it Alex still caught sight of a face peering at him from inside, and when he walked into the building through the heavy oak door and down the ancient hallways with all their skewed doorways, he often spotted something hiding that disappeared as soon as he approached it. The stairs were creaky and steep; the windows were old glass so that everything seen through them was wavy and twisted. It was a history museum so it was about dead people anyway, with stuff like the wicker casket on the second floor. Years ago, the casket was used to store a corpse until the weather warmed, the snow melted, the frozen earth thawed and the body could be buried. Every time Alex and his main man, Coker, passed it, they checked to be sure there was no one in there, forgotten, still waiting to be entombed. That's where the murderer should have put Aggie's body. That would have made sense. Alex and Coker had sworn never to be in the museum alone, especially after the sun set, since there was almost no electricity, just a light bulb and outlet in the closet on the first floor and another in the fourth floor library. The sheriff speculated that Mrs. Hamilton was murdered very early in the morning, just as night was turning to dawn. When all the shadows, gone in the blackness of the night, returned.

In the kitchen, with the butter churn and all the other cooking exhibits, there was a hole in the floor that was part of the cistern that Reverend Timothy Evensong, the man who built the Old Shrubsbury School House, devised to collect rainwater. If the wicker casket was too many stairs up for the killer to carry the body, the cistern was right there, next to the churn. It was big enough so he wouldn't have had to stuff her in. Whoever killed her either didn't know the kitchen very well or hated Old Aggie and her butter making so much they put her in the churn out of sheer malice.

Alex would have liked to offer that and other pertinent information to the sheriff, but the man didn't even ask him questions. He knew it was because he was a kid. The only grown-up at the museum who treated him with any respect was Ms. Mulholland who was an old lady and lived with her one-eyed cat on the second floor of the Cyril Benning House next door to the museum. She was the caretaker of the entire complex—a bunch of buildings, fifty-five acres and a lookout point. Because Alex's mother worked most days, and didn't want him to be home alone—even though he was so mature for his age it was nauseating—she found him a place at the museum doing odd jobs. He'd spent the summer hanging out with Ms. Mulholland, which was why he knew the place so well—well enough probably to solve Old Aggie's murder.

The Old Shrubsbury School House Museum wasn't like other places. It belonged to another century. The oak and maple trees that stood sentinel over the dirt roads, the antique houses, the wide green lawns, the watercolor white church and its cemetery, all the old and odd things, belonged to the past and the students who lived and studied there. Then, the village was on a stagecoach route from Boston to Canada. That was when it mattered. It was hard for Alex—who was very much of the present and had a taste for the future, for super heroes and interplanetary warfare—to spend the summer of his twelfth year in a time warp. Nonetheless, he'd gotten to know some of the students who attended the academy, long dead though they were, and most of them when they were alive, older than he was. High school students: Don Carlos Baxter, Horace Conant, Sarah Seavey, Thankful Smith... Ms. Mulholland showed him each of their rooms.

The museum was built as a dormitory for them in the 1830s by Reverend Evensong, one of the first African Americans to earn a college degree. Even though Vermont was just about the whitest state in the United States and still is today, Alex knew all about slavery and besides, there were three African American students in his school. Evensong who, in his daguerreotype, wasn't nearly as black as they were, looked very grim, but Alex had grown fond of the old sourpuss since, despite his appearance, he'd had a sense of humor. Besides, he was sort of a super hero, albeit the kind that lived in the past. Like Johnny Appleseed and Paul Bunyan, his life was the stuff of legends. It was said that he built the school building alone, using either a wooden or an earthen staging that rose as the building rose, his only helper an ox that worked an animal power to raise each massive granite block into place. When the last stone was finally hauled to the top, the ox wouldn't, or couldn't, come down—so the town celebrated the new building with an ox roast. That was the last exciting thing to happen in Shrubsbury. It had taken until now, almost two centuries later, for there to be another.

II

The baby in the portrait

R iding like the wind, jumping his Schwinn over ruts and mud holes, Alex headed straight for the museum on the day after the murder. It hadn't been easy getting his mother to say "go"—"Ms. Mulholland needs me," he told her, "I left her high and dry yesterday." But really, he wanted to talk about the murder. He had ideas. Leaving his bike on the chiseled stone porch, taking two steps at a time to the fourth floor, he found Ms. M weaving green and gold place mats on the barn loom while she waited with Adrian Dabney for a tour group. The tour had been scheduled months ago or old Dab wouldn't have opened up on the day after the murder.

"Hours, literally, it took hours on the telephone to persuade the silly woman to keep quiet about where we found the body. You know her," Adrian whined. "She thinks her newspaper is the *Times* of the Northeast Kingdom. All the news that's fit to print. But this isn't fit, not even remotely. It's all sooooo loathsome. We don't want tourists to stop coming to the museum. Do you have any idea what our checkbook looks like this time of year? Thank God, it's almost fall. In another month we can shut down for the winter and cut expenses. Next spring, pray God, it will be as if it never happened."

Tasha Mulholland nodded, put on her "It's going to be okay, Adrian" expression, and winked at Alex. Now, he could chill; Ms. Mulholland was the same. Aggie's death hadn't weirded her out. He shouldn't have worried. He'd forgotten that she could weave on the top floor all by herself, with the wind wailing and murky forms unfurling around the room. "I'm too old to be scared," she'd told him. Awesome.

Downstairs the tour group was tromping around. Adrian didn't see Alex on the other side of the loom, listening. He'd have stopped talking if he had since Alex was a child and Adrian was the kind of grown-up who didn't talk about death in front of children. Or sex. Although in this instance that was beside the point. Even though it didn't matter what Alex thought, since no one listened to him, it seemed to him that the murder should be front page news. Kids, even grown-ups, would freak out. They'd want to come. History could be such a bore. The murder would change that: museum attendance would soar; museum support would go through the roof.

When Adrian Dabney left, Alex sat on the bench with Ms. Mulholland while she wove. He waited until she was at the end of one movement and the beginning of the next, to ask her, "So who do you think did it?"

She stopped abruptly and looked down at him. She knew things that no one else did. Her son, Stuart Mulholland, was the county sheriff and he'd probably already told her stuff. Besides, people liked to tell her things because she listened. Ms. Mulholland would make a perfect partner if he was going to try to solve the crime. If the murderer was unlikely to suspect a kid, he'd never dream that he was being investigated by a kid and an old lady. Ms. Mulholland pressed down with her feet on the treadles at the bottom of the loom again and passed the shuttle back and forth through the shed opening.

"Why do you want to know, Alex?"

"Because I want to find the murderer."

She stopped again. "You know, even though almost no one liked her, it's still sad she's dead." She got a look on her face like something tasted bad.

"I didn't like her, but I don't like that someone did that to her."

"We'll talk after they leave," she said. The tour group was stomping up the last flight of stairs. "Maybe you and I could help solve her murder. What an odd pair of detectives we'd make. I'll make up a batch of chocolate chip cookies. That should help us think."

Alex slid off the bench and went to sit in the middle of the tall clocks at the center of the room. Lori Chickering was at the head of the group. Thin like a broomstick with hair like the broom part, she laughed too much—a horse laugh, and usually there was nothing funny—but as silly as she was, she and Alex got along. "Everybody, I want you to meet Mrs. Tasha Mulholland, our master weaver. She'll show you this floor." Lori started to leave, but stopped, remembering, and whirled around to point. "And Alex," she neighed. Alex felt his cheeks get hot. The tourists bobbed their heads at him, then gathered around to listen to Ms. Mulholland.

When she finished the weaving demonstration, she took the group to an exhibit on carding and spinning. Alex knew it all by heart. Someday he'd surprise her and do it—card wool, spin it, weave a place mat. Next, the tour group looked at the furniture, the hair wreaths made from real human hair—so gross, the old clocks, the portraits. He liked the room. The ceiling was very high, and there were small almost-as-high windows on three sides so that it felt like a tree house. Ms. Mulholland told the tour group how the students at the school used to sing and pray in this room. Matins, she said, and vespers too. Swaying, her voice rising and falling, she recited from a poem by a graduate.

> In reverie let me wander,
> Through dreamland wander o'er
> Again the scenes of girlhood
> In happy days of yore.
> Bring me the old stone house,
> That pile of granite grim;
> Lead me through its ancient halls
> And up the stairways dim.

Worn by many a footfall
Of noble, good and true;
Who roam in pain no longer
The paths that tears bedew.
In that bright parlor leave me,
Built there so near the sky,
Where silver moonbeams, mellow,
Shine through the windows high…
But listen, 'tis the pealing, low,
Of yonder silvery bell;
Like music stealing o'er me
With sweet and thrilling knell.

The poem was sappy; the parts she didn't say were worse. But it proved his point. The Old Shrubsbury School House Museum was haunted and always had been.

While the tour group moved from one site to another and Ms. Mulholland's voice hummed on, Alex studied his two favorite paintings: primitive portraits of Dr. Gerald Whittington and his wife, Juliette, who lived down and across the road in the Hamilton House where Old Aggie resided until yesterday morning, only back in 1834 when the house was brand new. Old Aggie always bragged that she was related to Juliette Whittington. Her great-great-great-ancestor was Juliette's sister. Most people paid little attention to her claims, or cared. Alex, however, had always admired the Whittingtons, despite their apparent connection to Aggie. Gerald was handsome and looked like 007 in his black suit. Juliette, also in

black, looked like a movie star in one of the sad historical movies
his mother favored. And there they were, side by side, the perfect
parents for him if he'd lived then. Alex's father had left when he
was a baby and his mother didn't really fit him. Even though he'd
never said it aloud, she was just too sloppy. Sweat pants. Dishev-
eled hair. Plump. Gazing at Juliette as sunlight caught her like a
spotlight, feeling guilty for his thoughts about his mother, Alex saw
something he'd never seen before. He blinked and it wasn't there
after all. He blinked again, and it was. A baby—a little indistinct
but nonetheless, a baby—was sitting on Juliette's lap, looking out
at the man who was painting the picture. An old-fashioned baby
with a round serious face like some of the dolls in the toy room.
"Where in the name of all that's holy," as Ms. M would have put
it, had she come from?

He could only see the baby from a certain angle, just from
where he was standing. When he moved in either direction, she
faded and was only the same dress and writing desk she'd been
for years. He saw her best when he squinted. She was probably
a girl but sometimes baby boys were dressed the same way, so he
couldn't be sure. When Ms. Mulholland took everyone into the
library across the hall, Alex got a chair and stood on it, since the
painting was hung high and he wanted to get as near as he could. It
was harder to see the image close up, so close to the brush strokes,
but the baby was definitely there. Why hadn't anyone ever noticed
her before? Why hadn't he?

Alex was still standing on the chair when Ms. Mulholland
came back into the room. "What, may I ask, are you doing up

there, Alexander Churchill?"

"Just looking at the painting. There's a baby in it. Did you know that?"

She looked at him like he was crazy so he got down from the chair and took her over to the side where she could see the round-faced child for herself. "I'll be darned. There is a baby," she said, shaking her head. "That's amazing. As if the painting's given birth. We should let Adrian know as soon as possible." She made a broad circle in front of the painting twice and came back again. "Well, maybe not today—he's in such a state."

"How can there be a baby now when there wasn't before?"

"It's hard to tell just by looking whether or not Juliette knows the child is there, the way she would have if they'd both been painted at the same time, but chances are they were painted together and she's been there all along. She must have been painted out for some reason. Maybe she died. Now the paint is fading and the image is beginning to show again."

Alex drew what seemed to him an obvious conclusion: "She got painted out and now she's come back. She's Aggie's relative and she came back. She's why Old Aggie was murdered."

Tasha Mulholland studied the painting for what seemed like a long, long time. "It is odd, isn't it, that the baby's only beginning to show again now?" She took the chair and put it back against the wall. "Try not to say 'Old Aggie,' Alex. It's not nice, even if she is dead."

III

The investigation begins

Since the first floor of Tasha Mulholland's house was the museum's research library, the place, top and bottom, smelled like old books. Even the cat and the cat's litter had a slight literary scent. Only two years older than the Old Shrubsbury School House, the Cyril Benning House had the same rolling floors and wavy windows. Cyril Benning Esq., the man who built it, was much too uninteresting to have left a ghost behind, as were all the people who'd lived in the house after him. Disappointing, but probably just as well. It made for a kind of serenity, Ms. M thought, which couldn't help but be a good thing at her age. The upstairs apartment was small with walls in earth tones, and cluttered with interesting things like a globe, lightly clad statuary from foreign countries, paintings, and books, all of it from her past adventures. There was also a cello that was too large for the place.

Because she was sixty-six years old, very modest and sometimes dithered, most people never gave Ms. M much thought.

She was lean and too tall for a woman, especially a woman of her years, and one who lived in such a small space. She was given to striding, not walking. Her dark bobbed hair was striped with silver and her cheeks were accented with a natural blush—apple cheeks her husband used to say. Her chin was a little too prominent and her mouth too large. Only someone who loved her would call her beautiful. She frequently wore an expression no one could interpret, or so she'd been told. She hoped that it made her seem inscrutable, since her thoughts were often odd ones she'd just as soon not share. Except when she wore nineteenth century costumes or attended funerals and weddings, she dressed in blue jeans, lacy shirts and comfortable shoes.

About the dithering, children visiting the Old Shrubsbury School House Museum sometimes laughed at her because she forgot her place and wandered verbally from one subject to another, but Alex didn't. He and Tasha Mulholland had become friends because he was smart and wanted to be smarter, and because he'd discovered that she knew all sorts of things he needed to know. She wasn't sure whether it was only a stage or something genetic and ongoing, but as long as that's where he was at, she was happy to be his adult friend. They argued, of course—mostly about superheroes versus stodgy historic characters like Evensong. Alex couldn't understand her love of the past and she couldn't fathom his absorption in make-believe futures with fanciful luminaries flying about to rescue women and whole metropolises.

Living next door to the Old Shrubsbury School House

Museum wasn't something Tasha Mulholland had planned on doing. She liked the place well enough, but being caretaker to a historical site was an accident. For her the museum was a compromise with fate: she lived rent free with plenty of time to think and play the cello after she mowed the acres of lawn around the buildings and supervised whatever volunteer workers she could find. She got to explore the lives of other people, most of them already dead, but even so with good stories. Her most profound ambition had always been to write philosophical tomes about the meaning of life and death, but by now she was aware that was unlikely. The wider world might just have to get along without.

There was no question she felt a little out of the loop, as if there were more leftover life to be lived than she was living. She'd stopped having exceptional adventures some years before, after she'd divorced her husband. Together they'd scaled pyramids on two continents and gone for long Nepalese treks; they'd lived through an African civil war and danced at a royal wedding, then made films about both. Their lives had been intoxicating and they'd both drunk deeply. But after they came home together the last time, after their son was born, her husband had looked for thrills in more conventional places and fallen into a tawdry affair that broke her heart.

She'd made a so-so living selling real estate—the Northeast Kingdom of Vermont was too remote to be a really desirable market—and raised the boy on her own. Life became very undramatic. Neither she nor Stuart had gotten ill with anything life threatening; there'd been no automobile accidents or natural disasters, no house fires. The boy was average in most ways and quite cheerful about it. When he grew up he looked for his own excitement in a job in law enforcement and quickly became sheriff—no one else was interested since in this part of Vermont a crime spurt usually meant no more than a few more traffic tickets or marijuana patches, an inebriated farmer, or petty thievery at the local drugstore. He married a hairdresser who was one of the shallowest people on the planet, or so it seemed to Tasha, and there were no grandchildren. But now, amazing as it seemed, she and her son were knee-deep in murder. It didn't surprise her that so far she was much more engaged by it than he was.

Tasha Mulholland was aware that she'd taken Alex on as a surrogate grandson—and that she'd better proceed with caution. Blood was thicker than water. If his mother decided to pick up and leave with Alex in tow, she could lose him and not have a word to say about it. Nonetheless, while she was a little disappointed in her own life, and her son's, she found herself hoping for more from Alex Churchill.

Solving a murder seemed a little beyond the pale to her, but then again she and Alex were both people who thought they could do anything. Normally, she wouldn't partner with a child in a murder investigation. As if there were anything normal about murder. And Alex hadn't just broached the possibility of working together, he'd discovered something that might be central to the mystery. Besides, it was apparent that he'd try to solve the crime no matter what she did. By himself he could get into real trouble. If they worked together, she might be able to save him from injury. Finally, apart from all these cautionary notes, his nimble mind complemented what she liked to think of as her riper intellect, and his computer savvy filled in gaps in her education. He was a child no one paid much attention; she was a past middle-aged lady they scarcely noticed. Between them, they just might be able to do it. They might solve the crime.

While Ms. M mixed up some chocolate chip dough in a bowl, and scooped out a dozen cookies, Alex brushed Winky, an ugly single-eyed feline no matter how hard he tried to fix her, with bald spots and ungainly posture for a cat. Ms. Mulholland put the cookie tins in the oven; Alex licked the bowl clean.

"We must be methodical," suggested Ms. M, and they made it his word for the day. Alex learned a word every day he worked with Ms. M since he was out to acquire smarts. He was working on a reputation as a brain, no mean feat when he had to do it without becoming a nerd. He was pretty sure that no adult, not even Ms. M, would understand that he had to solve this murder—and so he had no intention of explaining to her that it might be his once-in-a-lifetime opportunity to enhance his reputation, to transform himself into that rare anomaly, so rare as to be almost freaky, a guy who was both smart and cool.

"We came into the kitchen, I remember. It was about nine o'clock," Ms. Mulholland said. "There were a lot of us. You, me, your mother, Adrian Dabney, Lori Chickering, and some board members—Harold Plumbwell, Nick Crafts...Who else, Alex?"

"Major Shelton and Mrs. Shelton."

"Yes. Aggie had invited three board members, we don't know why, in addition to Adrian, probably because he's the director, and Lori, I suppose, because she's the director's assistant. And me because I'm the caretaker. Mrs. Shelton was there because of the Major; your mother was there by accident because she had a late day at her job at the store and had just brought you. No one knew why Aggie asked us to come—actually, as I remember—demanded it. She said it was vital to the future of the Old Shrubsbury School, and since we all hoped she'd leave her house and her money to the museum, we came."

"And then she never showed."

"Hmmmmm. Yes. I wonder if Adrian will put the barrel churn back in the kitchen." She got up to check the cookies, then sat down again, her chin resting in one hand while she doodled spirals on a stray napkin with the other. "You and I were the first to enter the kitchen. We were all surprised Aggie wasn't there, and we were annoyed. But of course we were glad at the same time, hoping she'd changed her mind. Adrian followed us. Since he had keys to the door, he could have been there earlier, certainly as early as she was. He hated her. Do you remember if he acted oddly, Alex?"

"He always acts oddly."

"Well, yes, I suppose he does," she said thoughtfully. "The board members followed him..."

"They were laughing at him because he was fussing about whether anyone had cleaned up the cluster flies. The Major was walking like a lady with a dust cloth."

"You're right. I wonder if Adrian even noticed." She pulled out a tin of cookies to check them, then eyed him narrowly. "What about the board members? What do we know about them? Not much, I think. I'll try to find out more by asking around. What did you think of them? How about the Sheltons? "

"The Major's a dork. His hair is dyed the most awful orange and his wife looks like she should be his daughter. She's silly like a kid. She's always telling him how good he is at everything. I'll bet he's not."

"My goodness, Alex. You gleaned all that in such a short time?"

"Before you got there we were waiting with them on the porch for Mr. Dabney to come with the keys. Why is Shelton called a Major anyway? He doesn't wear a uniform or anything."

"I think he's called a Major because he was one and now he's retired."

"He thinks he's uber everything."

"Well, I know that Agatha Hamilton disliked the Sheltons, especially Mrs. Shelton. She had a horror of limp women. Also of good looking women. I haven't an idea in the world why she invited them. Especially both of them. How about Harold Plumbwell?"

"Another dork. He's the principal at our school."

"I'd forgotten that. Is he a good principal?"

"Nope. Plumbwell's freakin' strict and not nice at all. But he and Mrs. Hamilton knew each other pretty good. I remember they talked for a long time on Old School House Day. I was doing my boy peddler act and tried to sell them apples. They both went bonkers like I'd interrupted something important. They sat on the stone wall in front of the building and yelled at each other the whole time the band played."

"I remember now. They were waving their arms around as if they were conducting the music. I expect he's not musical at all. He doesn't look like a person of rhythm. He wasn't happy, was he?"

"She really pushed him around. She made him get her rhubarb punch and a piece of boysenberry pie. Like she couldn't do it for herself."

"I wonder what they argued about."

"I wish I'd listened now, but then I just wanted to get away from them."

"How about Nick Crafts?"

"He's uber cool."

"He is, isn't he? He knows so much about history and he presses a fabulous apple."

"I don't know if he and Mrs. Hamilton ever even talked."

"Well, I happen to know that they knew each other very well. At least in a certain sense."

"Whadayamean?"

"His father and Mrs. Hamilton were lovers years ago."

"Oh, man. Crazy."

22

"Back then, Agatha was good looking. I'll find some pictures downstairs and show you." She could see he didn't quite believe it, but he was trying. Removing wrinkles and pale hanging flesh. Inserting long dark hair over a scraggly gray mop.

"She couldn't be Nick Crafts' mother, could she?"

"I don't think so, but that was before my time. Do you remember how he acted when we found the body?"

"Yeah. He looked as if he was going to puke."

"Hmmmmm. What about Lori Chickering?"

"She was wacko like she usually is. She came in wearing sweats and Nikes because she'd been running and counting bluebirds' nests. Then she kept interrupting Mr. Dabney, asking dumb questions."

"She didn't understand the butter churn, she said."

"Yeah. She asked how it worked. And when you asked me to help turn the handle to show her…"

"…we ended by opening it. Odd. She must have known how it worked. But maybe she was trying to impress Nick Crafts."

"How would that impress him?"

"Just impressing him with her presence, letting him know she was there. He's very handsome, Alex."

"But she's not pretty, even a little bit. And she's too weird. Anyway, she has keys like Mr. Dabney. She could have been there early. And no alibi because she was off running."

"Alibis. I almost forgot about alibis. Sometimes I'm glad for all your TV. Let's see. He said he came straight from home and

23

since his wife has left him, no one else would have been there."

"The Major said he and Mrs. Shelton had just come from refinishing a melodeon. Can you believe it? Like he thought they might need an alibi."

"It would have been easier for two people to have done the crime, wouldn't it?"

"Oh, yeah."

"What about your principal, Alex?"

"Another guy who announced his alibi without anyone asking for it, or thinking he should have one. He said he'd just come from the school where he'd been cleaning blackboards."

"That's right. Your school starts tomorrow, doesn't it?"

"Yeah. It's a drag." He knew she sympathized with him. He was usually unhappy there anyway—it was so dull. His mother and Tasha both thought he was too bright for Shrubsbury Elementary School and, maybe, for any school anywhere.

"So Principal Plumbwell's alibi can be checked, I guess. At least if anyone helped him with the blackboards. What about Nick Crafts?"

"I don't know. He didn't say anything. He looked bored until you opened the churn."

Ms. Mulholland counted out six cookies and slid them onto a plate, then poured Alex a glass of milk and herself a cup of coffee. A devoted coffee drinker, she usually drank a flavor and strength appropriate to the day, which on this day meant a variety called Jungle Madness. "This should help," she said with a sigh, raising the cup to her lips, then looking at Alex seriously, swallowing, hesitating. "Alex, let's talk about our detective work for a minute. I don't think your mother would be glad to know you're doing this."

"No, ma'am. She wouldn't. But I don't have to tell her. She likes it when I spend time with you because she says I always learn so much."

"This will certainly be a learning experience. Did you have nightmares about Mrs. Hamilton?"

"No, but I woke up a lot. Since I didn't like her, I don't know why what happened to her feels so bad. I guess it's just that murder is yuckier than I thought it would be."

"Do you think you'll feel better if we find out who did it?"

"Yep. Otherwise, it's like a story with no end. It stays all messed up. Anyway, they solve murders on TV all the time. I've studied how they do it, and it doesn't look that hard."

"I think it's going to be harder than it is on TV. And we're going to make sure it's a whole lot safer. I'll only make a partnership with you if you agree safety is our first priority. We won't tell a soul. Not only would my son not approve of an elderly woman doing this and your mother not approve of her boy doing it, we'll stay safer if no one knows. We're going to have to be a secret partnership."

How cool was that? He'd been worried that his mother wouldn't like his being a detective. Just as bad, he knew some of the kids would make him out to be a wimp working with an old lady like Ms. Mulholland. As for the staying safe stuff, he'd wait and see. You probably couldn't stay too safe looking for a murderer.

"Yo, Ms. M. What do we do next?"

"I'm not sure, but we want to know what Aggie was going to tell us since she may have been killed because of it. So why don't we do research? We'll use our own special talents. You'll do research on the internet, and I'll do research in the library downstairs and in the town clerk's office. What do you think?"

Even better. Alex was a computer wizard. "What are we looking for?"

"First, we'll look for Mrs. Hamilton's genealogy. We don't know that there's a connection between the painting and the murder, but there could be. Aggie spent a lot of time working on her genealogy. I can find it in the library downstairs—probably several versions of it—but I remember her talking about a website, and that may be where we'll find the most recent version."

"So if we can find out who the baby was and how she was related to the Whittingtons and to Mrs. Hamilton, we might figure out what she called the meeting for, and why someone would want to kill her."

"Hmmmmm. Although, there's already an obvious motive."

"Money."

"Exactly. I'll try to find out who inherits Mrs. Hamilton's house and money. Adrian might know. I'll catch him tomorrow and start him talking—that's never hard to do. I imagine her daughter gets everything, but we'll see."

"Maybe her daughter killed her."

"She lives in Boston. They didn't get along, but I don't think she was around." She got up and walked to the window. "Alex, look for all our suspects on the internet. Sometimes people are up to the strangest things, especially there. And include Aggie's daughter. Her name's Serendipity."

"Serendipity? What kind of name is that?"

"It's not unlike your generation's expression: 'Whatever.' Whatever Hamilton. But everyone calls her Sera."

She stared out across the road at Agatha Hamilton's house. "Why don't we forget the window washing today. Shall we go fishing?"

IV

Blood and gore

Ms. Mulholland didn't usually like to fish: it seemed like a cruel thing to do to worms and fish, but Alex took care of the most barbaric aspects of it, and there was something relaxing about sitting on a rock with a pole.

Today, however, neither she nor Alex could stop thinking about murder.

"What about it, Ms. Mulholland? Where did the murderer kill her? They found the bread knife that killed her in the churn with the fingerprints wiped clean, but they didn't find the murder scene, did they?"

"Seems like there'd be lots of blood at the murder scene, doesn't it, Alex?"

"Yep. But there was hardly any blood in the kitchen that I could see."

"According to my son, there was a little on the outside of the churn, and a bit smeared on the kitchen door frame. None of it in the form of readable fingerprints."

"On the kitchen door to outside?"

"Yes. But nowhere else."

"That's gotta mean the killer did it outside."

"Maybe. As soon as we catch something, shall we go look for a murder scene?"

They didn't wait that long. Soon, they put down their poles and walked back to the museum, slowly, neither of them saying anything, not really eager to see the kitchen again. Tasha Mulholland found herself acutely conscious of how very tall she was and how short Alex was—a tall, elderly woman and a puny red-headed kid with freckles. What was she thinking? His voice hadn't even changed.

They walked round and round the building studying the close-cut green grass, looking for the impress of a bloody body, grass mashed down, blades of grass tipped in red, anything bloody. They looked in the Education Center. They looked in the fields that bordered the museum grounds, they looked in Timothy Evensong's house, now the administration building for the museum.

The day was turning cloudy and rainy, the kind of autumn afternoon visitors were unlikely to turn up, and Adrian had locked up the museum. Because she was the caretaker, Ms. Mulholland had the keys to everywhere, and since Alex liked unlocking the huge oak door at the front, she handed him the big skeleton key that opened it. It went into the keyhole loosey goosey— That's how Tasha Mulholland described it—and you had to turn it just right for it to catch and turn the metal.

Inside, light and shadows were taking turns in the building and it was hard to know how to feel from one minute to the next. They went straight down the hallway to the kitchen, but stopped at the yellow ribbon strung across the doorway. Alex's stomach felt queasy and when Ms. Mulholland took hold of his hand he was glad. "It's unsettling to be here again," she said. She squeezed his fingers tight.

"But there's nothing to be scared of," Alex said bravely. "Wouldn't Mrs. Hamilton make an awful ghost?" They both laughed but not too hard because it wasn't as funny as it would have been if she were still alive.

They ducked under the tape and went into the kitchen, but stopped again in the middle of the room while Ms. Mulholland rummaged in her pockets for the two pairs of white cotton gloves she always carried. Usually, she and Alex wore them to protect old objects from their sweaty palms, but today they wanted to preserve any fingerprints the sheriff might have missed. They walked around looking for more blood, peering into the beehive oven with flashlights, gazing down into the cistern and into the built-in sink on the other side of the fireplace. They examined all the butter making equipment. There wasn't a drop of blood anywhere. Finally, with no place else to look, they sat down on two small chairs by the cupboard, and Ms. Mulholland asked the obvious question: "How could someone carry Aggie into the room all the way from outside and jam her into the butter churn without blood getting on something?"

"I don't know. But she had to have been killed outside," Alex said.

"That's what Stuart believes."

"But you don't think so."

"It's a long distance from the door to the churn. They didn't find any blood outside, and neither did we. I know the world outside is wide, wide as all outdoors, but even so... Still, Stuart searched everywhere in the building that makes sense, and didn't find a trace of blood."

They sat quietly looking at the kitchen fireplace, listening to the wind hugging the oak trees and seeing the inhabitants of the school of more than a century ago begin preparations for dinner: The cook sitting on a small painted chair, peeling potatoes for the dinner meal; Mercy Evensong humming a hymn tune as she prepared a freshly plucked duck for the oven; Thankful opening up the root cellar to find butter to smear on the naked white bird, and the milk and eggs gathered that morning for a sauce.

"There is one place," Ms. Mulholland said, "that I've been afraid to look at again. It seemed to me that Stuart didn't really search the root cellar. It is, after all, right next to where the butter churn stood. Adrian told him it's empty, with only one small window near the ceiling, with the door to the outside barred on the inside. Besides all that, the sheriff's mother is the only person who has the key to the door from the kitchen. So they borrowed my key. It took two sturdy men to get it open because the door was warped from the years it's been closed. They flashed a light around and didn't see anything. They closed it up again. And that was that."

"Are you the only person with a key?" Alex asked.

"I doubt it," said Ms. Mulholland. The building was quieter than Alex could remember, and he held his breath when she put the key in the lock and turned it. It made a loud click. It still wasn't easy to budge the door, but after a few minutes they managed to push it open to the pitch black inside. "Good of them to loosen it for us," Ms. Mulholland said. "Why don't you go get the lantern from the closet so we have better light?"

Gingerly, she stepped down from the kitchen to the root cellar's dirt floor and onto one of the boards that lay across it. Alex followed close behind, nervously swinging the lantern around the gray musty walls. The room smelled of damp stones, dirt, and something else—he didn't know what but he didn't like it. A century ago, the root cellar was used to store milk, butter and vegetables. It wasn't the least bit sinister then. It was just a big refrigerator. It had been closed up for so long, Alex figured, not even rats and spiders lived in it now. He shone the light down onto the dirt floor and the crusted planks that crisscrossed it. Just dirt. It was all dirt. Ms. Mulholland stooped down and drew a line on one of the planks with her finger. She held it up in the lantern beam. On her gloved fingertip was something red that looked like blood.

"I'll tell Stuart," she said. "The murderer must have killed Mrs. Hamilton in this room." Alex threw the light around for her again and their shadows rose up on the stone walls like spectres in a horror movie. "I wonder if there's something else we're not seeing," she added.

"Does the door to the outside still open?" Alex asked. "We could open it and make more light."

"I'm sure it does." She stepped down onto the dirt floor and he set the lantern down on the plank. Together they struggled to remove the wooden bars that held the door shut. They wriggled each bar loose and propped it up against the wall, then pulled the door open until daylight poured in.

They could see now—and what they saw was that they'd been standing in Aggie's sticky blood. "In the name of all that's holy," muttered Ms. Mulholland, making for the outside with Alex a step behind her. They flopped onto the damp grass and sat, gazing silently, grimly, into the cellar space.

"It's hard to think about Mrs. Hamilton getting killed in there," Tasha Mulholland said at last, almost as if she could read Alex's thoughts. "She wouldn't have had any place to run."

"Yeah," Alex said and swallowed hard. "But I bet she screamed as loud as she could. If her sound was stuck in that room it must have made the guy who killed her crazy."

They imagined Aggie spitting and sputtering in the small dark space, saw her opening her mouth wide, heard her screaming into the lantern-lit darkness of the little room, the sound thrashing from one stone wall to another as the killer raised the bread knife...

"Are you okay, Alex?"

"Yeah. Just kind of grossed out." She handed him a clean tissue from her pocket and took another for herself, but she didn't say anything. She didn't even say anything about her incompetent son, the sheriff. The only thing she did say, finally, was, "What in the world was Agatha Hamilton doing in the root cellar?"

After they locked up everything, they went back to the apartment for more cookies. Ms. Mulholland asked Alex if he minded if she played the cello. It helped her cope. Of course he said "no" like it didn't matter one way or the other to him. The truth was he was afraid it would make him cry because sometimes it did even when he wasn't weirded out. He loved to listen to her, sometimes he even needed to, but he would never say it aloud because his favorite band was Beastie Boys. He wasn't at all sure that a boy of twelve with serious deficits in soccer, trouble-making and all-round coolness should be listening to a cello with his eyes full. So he sat with his back to her, stroking Winky, trying hard not to listen to the solemn Bach sonata she played, watching the tops of maples blowing in the wind out the window. He left as soon as it seemed polite to murmur "goodbye" and pedaled down the road as fast as he could, not home, not yet, just around until he got tired.

V

The cool side of murder

It was a downer being back in school. All Alex could think about was the murder. But the Force was with him—he'd acquired a rep. At recess everyone, even some of the eighth graders, collected to hear him tell about finding Agatha Hamilton's corpse in a butter churn. Every report card since kindergarten he'd been "a quiet, modest boy"—or, translation—a boring guy in a dull school in a duller town. At long last he was a righteous dude. This could be a banner year.

A crowd of kids walked with Alex to the ball field to hang out and listen, tossing a ball around like it was any other day, so they wouldn't be interrupted by teachers, or by Principal Plumbwell. Alex had stayed up late the night before, rehearsing this performance. Now, he took his time and when he began talking, he spoke so softly they had to come close and strain to hear.

"It was a stormy morning," he said, when they were all huddled around him. "Inside the academy, it was shadowy and creepy and we all stopped talking and listened to the wind slapping at the windows and the stairs creaking. It felt like something was wrong.

"We went to the kitchen because that's where Old Aggie had told us to go. There was me and my mom, Ms. Mulholland, geeky Director Dabney, Miss Chickering, and a few other grown-ups. One of them was someone we all know and love."

He rolled his eyes back towards the school. "Who?" they asked. "Tell us, who?" "You mean Principal Plumbwell?" someone guessed." "Hey, Bummer Plumbwell was there?" someone else said. Another kid snickered: "Bet he did it!" They all laughed. "He's a suspect like everyone else," Alex said gravely.

"Old Aggie was supposed to be there, but she wasn't—or so we thought," Alex added, and everyone laughed again, but this time uneasily. "When we came into the kitchen, Director Dabney suggested that we talk about something historical while we waited for Old Aggie, like maybe the root cellar or the barrel churn. Miss Chickering asked how the barrel churn worked. Ms. M was going to show her and tried to turn the handle. But it wouldn't move, and I couldn't make it move either. Something clunked inside when I tried." He paused to let them wonder what it was.

"Ms. Mulholland thought it might be a practical joke by the high school kids and we'd open it up and find a pair of smelly Nikes or maybe rocks because it seemed so heavy. It was hard to get the cover loose. Someone had really jammed it on." He paused for a long moment and took a deep breath.

"It wasn't Nikes. It wasn't rocks," he said, and paused again, but for a shorter time. His timing was wicked.

"It was Old Aggie."

Some kids gasped; someone muttered "gross"; a girl giggled. He waited for a perfect stillness. "Her feet were on either side of her face"—he put his hands up like they were feet with his head between them—"because the murderer had to fold her in two to get her in."

Everyone stirred uncomfortably and someone made yucky noises. Nellie, who he couldn't stand, clamped her hands over her ears and closed her eyes so she couldn't read his lips, as if she could read lips anyway. Someone else shushed and two of the guys threw the ball back and forth for a minute because Plumbwell was looking in their direction.

"One shoe was missing—that's what clunked—so one of her feet was bare. Her toes were little and pink with blood on them like messy nail polish." He wiggled the fingers on his right hand. "Her eyes bulged out of her head." He made his eyes wide and bugged them out. "Blood was all over her face and neck, and sticking in her hair. Her mouth was open like she was screaming." He opened his mouth, and held the pose.

Some of the girls covered their eyes. When he finally put his hands down, he could hear kids start breathing again.

"I couldn't stop looking at her even though Ms. Mulholland tried to get me to," he said, finishing his story as quietly as he'd begun it. "Finally my mom came and got me and I went outside and barfed."

Since he'd promised Ms. Mulholland not to talk about their detective work, he couldn't say more, not even about Plumbwell, but he could tell the kids thought the whole thing was off the hook, except for some of the girls, especially Nellie, who was plump and loud-mouthed and didn't matter anyway.

During lunch he revealed to Coker that Bummer Plumbwell didn't have an alibi, but only because Coker was his main man. They were sitting eating when the principal came wandering by and looked at him as if he knew he knew things. "He creeps me out," Alex muttered. "Me too," Coker replied. Coker wasn't a kid who was easily creeped. He was already bigger than Principal Plumbwell. At the rate he was growing he'd be able to take him soon, maybe even later this year.

Geography was one of Alex's areas of expertise since Ms. Mulholland and he had discussed the world many times during the summer, so he figured he could spend the class time on the subject thinking about the evidence he found on the computer the night before. Aggie's website was big with a lot of pages and links. His most important discovery was that Plumbwell had helped her with her latest genealogy. She gave him credit at the bottom. Since Old Aggie hadn't been a grateful sort of person, he wondered about that. Plumbwell, he was sure, wasn't the kind of guy who helped anyone unless there was something in it for him. He was a runt of a man with thinning hair and small light eyes, and a mouth that fell naturally into a sneer. He was about as well liked as Aggie had been. None of the teachers said anything, of course, but the kids could tell they couldn't stand him either.

Aggie had put some other stuff online too, like pictures of the furniture in her house, lessons on making butter, and a story about her ancestors, especially the people in the paintings in the Old Shrubsbury School. The baby wasn't in the picture of the painting and she didn't mention her.

"Alex, would you come up here and show us the continents? Alex? Are you awake?" Alex came to with a start. Some of the girls tittered. It wasn't as if he'd been snoring or anything. The teacher had apparently missed how cool he'd become. At the front of the room there was a world map spread out across the blackboard. He found North America, South America, Africa, Europe and Asia. He remembered Australia when the teacher said, "Think, Alex. Think. It begins with an A." But he didn't remember Antarctica. Smart alecky Nellie raised her hand and did it for him.

When he sat down again, an awesome question came to him. Why hadn't the murderer left Mrs. Hamilton in the root cellar? No one would have known she was there until she smelled. That could have been a long time, the room was so cold and winter was coming—maybe not until next summer. Maybe not for years. Leave it to this town to have a dumb murderer.

When the school day finally ended, Ms. Mulholland was in the parking lot in her yellow Ford truck waiting for him. It was fortunate he liked living dangerously because she was a really wicked driver. He was never sure they'd get where they were supposed to, although so far they had. His mother assumed Ms. M drove carefully because she was old, even if what she drove was yellow. As she ground the gears and the truck jerked forward, he put the question to her: why didn't the murderer leave Mrs. Hamilton in the root cellar? She smiled and shifted again, smoothly this time, and he knew she'd wondered too.

"Do you have any theories, Alex?"

"You mean besides his being dumb?"

"Yes."

"I guess he must have wanted everyone to know Mrs. Hamilton was dead."

"Probably. If someone just disappeared there might be problems with inheritance, or insurance."

"So for someone to get money, everyone needs to know the dead person is really dead?"

"Yes. But, on the other hand, maybe the murderer just wanted to brag that he'd killed her, and the butter churn was a good way to do that."

She took some sharp turns and they bounced through clouds of dust made white in the glare of the afternoon sun. "How come we didn't talk about Antarctica when we did the continents this summer?" Alex asked.

"You missed that one today, huh?"

"Yep."

"Well, we didn't because I didn't know there was much to know about it. Just ice."

Alex nodded. "Are we going to look in the root cellar again today?"

"No. I had to let Stuart know about it—he is the sheriff after all—so he and his minions searched it this afternoon."

"Downer. Did the minions find anything?"

"Look that word up when you get home. M-i-n-i-o-n-s. Yes, but not enough."

"Like what?"

"They found more blood, of course. And a footprint, recently made, belonging to a man, size nine shoe. So a man of smaller stature than most. A new and cheaply made shoe, Stuart thought, but a dress shoe, so no workman."

"Awesome. So no Miss Chickering. No Major's wife. No Nick Crafts. He wears boots. The Major is a big guy so his feet are probably big, but Bummer Plumber might be about the right size."

"Not Bummer, Alex. Someday you'll say that in the wrong place at the wrong time—but about the shoes, Principal Plumbwell might or might not fit them."

"Maybe it was a woman wearing shoes like a man like Coker's mother does sometimes? Or maybe the guy with the footprint was someone besides the murderer?"

"Yes. Could be. Or maybe one of Stuart's minions accidentally stepped the wrong place. That can happen. At any rate, he wasn't sure it was a clear enough print to go after anyone's shoes."

"So we don't really know much of anything."

"That's about it." She pulled into the driveway.

"Did they look for what Mrs. Hamilton was looking for? Like secret spaces in the stones? Or writing somewhere?"

"He said they did. If there's something there, it wasn't apparent."

Upstairs, Ms. Mulholland started by doing what she always did, pouring Alex some milk and herself a coffee. The flavor on this afternoon was called "Meditation." Alex guessed it was for a different kind of thinking than the day before. Ms. Mulholland brought the cookie jar over and set it on the table—clearly, they were going to need more cookies than ever.

"Alex," she said. "I wonder if we should keep investigating. That was pretty gruesome yesterday. Are you okay?"

"I'm fine. How about you, Ms. M?"

"I'm worried that the murderer might find us before we find him. I'd feel terrible if anything happened to you. Or to me, for that matter."

"You're chicken shit."

"Alex! Don't talk that way. We'll quit this minute if you're going to behave like that."

"I'm sorry," Alex said, not really meaning it.

"Anyway, I'm not, as you put it, 'chicken shit.' I think maybe I'm just not being very responsible doing this with you without your mother's permission."

"My mom is scared to leave me home alone in boring Shrubsbury. My mom is pretty much scared of everything. If you try to fire me from being your partner, I'll just keep looking on my own. You wouldn't want that, would you?"

"Blackmail. You're barely twelve and you're blackmailing me."

"Yep."

With a self-satisfied grin, Alex told her about his findings on the internet, and gave her copies of everything. There were so many pages he'd timed it so that he printed at the same time as his mother talked to his aunt. Because his aunt couldn't hear very well, their conversations were always loud and long.

"So Aggie didn't say anything about a baby? Nothing at all."

"No, ma'am."

"Well, there are several genealogies in the library that don't either. But I found one that says something different. I'm not sure who made it, but it was done about twenty-five years ago."

"They thought there was a child?"

"Yes, a baby girl named Isabelle."

"Did she die?"

"Not that I could discover, but the genealogy didn't follow her. Just named her. That was it. No descendants given. I'll look in the town's records tomorrow when the town clerk's office is open. I suppose she could be in one of those infant graves in the graveyard across the road."

"Should we go search?"

"It probably won't be of any use, but we could go over and look before it gets dark. There are some infant stones without any identification on them, where the baby died so soon after birth she wasn't even named. If there was an Isabelle, she seems to have lived long enough to be called that. Besides, the baby in Mrs. Whittington's portrait looks a few months old. But her body may be the same one the painter used for many other children. Just a generic nineteenth century infant's body."

She leaned back in her favorite chair and Winky jumped up to sit on her lap and purr. Usually they made bad jokes about how loud he was—gun the motor, Winky; gas up, cat, gas up—but this time they couldn't talk of anything but murder. "I also checked out alibis with Stuart. No one has one since the coroner says the time of death was five or earlier. Nick Crafts is the only person who owns up to being out and about at that hour. He rose early in the morning, probably about four-thirty, and ate a granola bar while he drove around waiting for daylight. He's looking for land to buy so after that he went from one piece of real estate to another until he met us in the kitchen."

"What if a stranger did it? Or someone who wasn't at the meeting?"

"It's possible, but it doesn't seem likely, does it? Since the murder probably had something to do with the meeting."

Alex pushed away his milk glass and peeled off the paper on a new bubble gum. One of the girls who'd pretended to be grossed out by his story gave it to him after school. Clearly, she wasn't that grossed out; clearly, she liked him. One of the perks that went with being cool. He lobbed the gum into his mouth. "Did your son know anything else?"

"No, at least not that he would tell me. But I learned a lot from Lori today. She surprised me."

"How'd she surprise you, Ms. M?" He clamped down hard on the new bubble gum, waiting for stories.

"When she first moved here, only a year and half ago now, Mrs. Hamilton took her under her wing, hoping, I thought at the time, for an ally against Adrian. You may not remember that. Anyway, they spent hours together talking about the history of the Old Shrubsbury School and Mrs. Hamilton's own history and ancestors. I don't think you quite know the story. It began with Juliette Whittington's father, Stephen West, living in Mrs. Hamilton's house in the 1830s, about the same time as Evensong was building the academy. He and his wife had another daughter named Audrey who was Mrs. Hamilton's great-great-great-grandmother." Ms. Mulholland pointed to Audrey on the family tree from the website. "Juliette and her husband, Gerald, moved into the house about 1838. While Juliette had no children, Audrey had two sons, and Aggie is the direct descendant of one of them. If Juliette had a child, Stephen's wealth when he died would have been split between Audrey and Juliette and half would have been passed down through Juliette's line to someone. But Juliette died young and childless.

"Mrs. Hamilton was emphatic that Juliette never had children. Family lore has it that she was deeply envious of her sister, and Mr. Whittington was so unhappy because he was childless he even talked about divorcing her, something nearly unheard of in that day. It was said that she died of a broken heart."

"Maybe Mrs. Hamilton just didn't want anyone to know

about Juliette's baby," Alex said, blowing a bubble and letting it pop. Ms. Mulholland started up ever so slightly.

"Could be. If there really was a baby. If she knew there was. We only have a little bit of evidence: one genealogy out of maybe a dozen, and a dim image in a painting. Let's not jump to conclusions. Besides, it's just as possible that if there was a baby, Aggie only found out about it when the image appeared in the painting."

"What else did Lori remember?"

"Once, when she was at Mrs. Hamilton's house having tea, your principal came over. Aggie told him she'd talk to him some other time and slammed the door in his face."

Your principal! Ha! As if he were responsible for Plumbwell. "Yo. Best thing she ever did."

VI

The ghost in the cemetery

It wasn't late, but the gray weather made it feel like it was almost night. Clouds were skittering across the sky and the trees were rattling with the first autumn leaves. Big black shadows played leapfrog in the graveyard. Early Halloween.

Both Ms. Mulholland and Alex knew the cemetery well. Alex had made rubbings at day camp of Reverend Evensong's stone. Before Alex had even been born, Ms. Mulholland had walked her dog, Effie, among the stones. Effie died of old age long ago and was buried on a hillside overlooking the graveyard. Since the Whittington graves were among Effie's favorites, Ms. M knew exactly where to begin.

The Whittington stones had flowers curlicued around the top and willow trees on the front. "Dr. Gerald Whittington," one stone said. "Born 1810. Died 1843. Resting in the Arms of Jesus." Next to him lay the beautiful Juliette. "Born 1812. Died 1841. At Peace at Last." Fat stones with soft edges, the graves seemed to

Alex to be all about tranquility. Gerald and Juliette were probably cradled in God's very large arms, smiling at each other. The way they didn't smile in their paintings. Ms. Mulholland had explained to him that people back then were supposed to look serious because it was such an important thing to be painted, but the Whittingtons might have looked grim anyway because they had broken hearts. Especially if their baby had died. Maybe she was with them now, curled up in their arms while they were curled up in God's. But, of course, if Mr. Whittington had been contemplating a divorce…

Once, when he was younger and asked uncomfortable questions all the time, Alex asked Ms. Mulholland if she wanted to be buried in this graveyard. "God, no," she replied. "Why not?" he asked. She'd spent so much time here, she answered him, she knew the people too well. "Somehow, even on the other side of the grave, I think I'd get claustrophobic." Usually, the graveyard didn't bother Alex, but Aggie's death made it feel different, like it was crowded with eerie personalities.

There were a few infant graves near the Whittingtons', but none of them seemed to belong to a Whittington baby. They found a gravestone for Audrey, her husband, and some of her descendants. While Ms. Mulholland checked them off on the genealogy, Alex wandered over to the new hole the grave digger had just finished making for Old Aggie. It was deep, dark and sweet-smelling; the sun had sunk so low he could barely see the bottom. The smell of newly turned earth made him think of his grandfather's funeral and the preacher intoning, "earth to earth, dust to dust." When he worried that his grandpa had dissolved into dirt, his mother said they always read that and not to worry. While it upset him to think of his grandfather turning to dirt, he liked the idea for Old Aggie. It was nice to think that she'd turned into something fresh and cool like the soil and that flowers might even grow from her.

He heard a sing-song voice from somewhere on the other side of the hole. Or was it from the inside? "Hello, there," it said, wavering in the wind. "The hole's dug, I see." It was like Old Aggie's voice only with harder edges, and colder. Even icy. Alex bent over the hole to make sure there was no one there. Nothing but darkness and dirt. Scary. He felt himself getting goose bumps; he couldn't swallow; he almost couldn't breathe. He opened his mouth to gulp in air and his bubble gum fell out and into the hole with an inaudible plop.

Where was Ms. Mulholland? When he looked up for her, slowly, carefully, he saw a strange figure in a long, black cloak standing on the other side of the grave against a blood red sky, the wind whipping the cloak—slap, slap, slap. "Hello," the voice said again. So it was her.

"It's good to see you again, Ms. Hamilton." said Ms. Mulholland, so mannerly, like she wasn't talking to a ghost at all.

"I've come for the funeral, of course." Weirder and weirder yet. The wind was blowing crows across the sky behind the woman who seemed to be growing larger. He twisted around to try and see Ms. Mulholland. He didn't know where to hide. Maybe she'd know. Climb a tree, head for the road, the church outhouse? Was any place safe from the ghost of Old Aggie?

"I'm so sorry about your mother, Sera."

Of course. "Whatever" Hamilton. He made himself stand up and stop shaking. No ghosts. Just the daughter of one.

"I hear that you were the one who found her, Tasha."

"Yes. I'm afraid it's true. Myself and this young man, Alex Churchill."

"It's kind of fitting she'd end up that way, but I am sorry you two had to be the ones to come across her."

"Why do you say 'fitting,' Sera?"

"She'd made so many enemies over the years. And a butter churn? Why not? Do you know I can't eat butter to this day?"

Alex saw Ms. Mulholland wince. What a terrible thing, not to be able to eat butter.

"I wouldn't be so blunt about her to just anybody. But you know what she was like."

"I'm afraid so. Do you have any idea who killed her?"

"No. Just about everyone wanted to."

"Will the house be yours now, Sera?"

"I don't know. There's far more than the house, of course—she had a bundle of money to unload. When they read the will, I guess we'll find out. She wasn't fond of me, you know—she disinherited me many times—but she did care about family lineage and all that."

"You don't think she would have passed the house at least on to the museum?"

"No. I don't think she would have left anything to the museum; she was too angry at everyone, especially Adrian."

"If you don't mind my asking, when are they planning to

read the will?"

"I suppose after the coroner's report and the funeral. I don't really know but probably sometime next week. Would you like to attend? You're as likely a beneficiary as anyone. You were always civil to her, Tasha. No one else can say that."

"Are you staying at the house?" They started walking together towards the gate with Alex trailing just behind. It squeaked like it hurt when Ms. Mulholland swung it open, closed it, and hooked it after them.

"Yes."

"Are you comfortable there?"

"God help me. It's a mess. Your sheriff son went through the place and made it even messier, but not by much. Mother had gotten dafter than ever, you know. Everything is just chaos. Paper everywhere. But still, yes, I am staying there, and I intend to stay as long as I can."

"Sera, you wouldn't consider letting me look around, would you? I know it's an imposition, but Alex and I are interested in Shrubsbury genealogies. And your mother spent so much time on them."

"Genealogies?" she raised her heavy eyebrows high. "I can't understand why you'd be interested, especially the boy. But you can look around. History this and that is everywhere. Some of it's probably genealogy."

"Maybe tomorrow afternoon, after Alex gets out of school?"

"Sure. Three-thirty or so? I'll give you tea. We can dis the old lady some more."

VII

An accumulation of clues

Alex despaired of his Civil War homework to his mother at supper and bookmarked a Civil War website so he could get to it fast if she came looking. He was really doing detective work. Nick Crafts, it turned out, had a Facebook page and a blog about coming home to Vermont and looking for real estate. He remembered living in Shrubsbury when he was a kid; his family moved to New York when he was seven. Living in New York had been great but he'd wanted to move back to rural Vermont even though the place had unsettled his father and mother. As well it might have if Old Aggie and Nick's father had an affair, Alex noted. Eerie, oh so eerie.

He couldn't find anything on Aggie's daughter, Serendipity. On Mrs. Hamilton's genealogy, she listed her daughter as an investment counselor, but even though he didn't know what that was, Alex doubted it. People who looked like her didn't do ordinary things: she had to be an actress or a fortune teller, or maybe a professional thief. She might even be in the circus.

The Major and his wife turned out to be more interesting than they looked. They were on eBay pushing antiques so they must know something about butter churns. The Major was trying to sell a melodeon (there were a bunch of those in the museum), some ugly old dolls, and a painting of a place that looked familiar but Alex couldn't say why. The caption said it was painted in 1838. He made a copy of it for Ms. Mulholland.

He was too excited to do his homework. Coker texted him about Principal Plumbwell: "hru uc plumer wtchg u?" Alex wrote back: "W/E." (Whatever.) He wished he could tell Coker he was investigating Bummer Plumber. Mostly Coker wanted to know if he did the math homework and what answer he got for number four. The year before they'd played Rune Scape almost every night; he didn't know if they would again this year. No way he could until the murder was solved.

Alex hit his Civil War bookmark and left it on at the same time as he tried to think about the Major. Just in time. His mom came from around the corner and looked over his shoulder, all hovering and helpful. "Anything I can do for you?" As if she knew anything about the Civil War.

"Nah. I'm okay. It's just hard to do homework again. More and more of it. It's Bummer Plumber's idea. He's trying to kill us."

"Mr. Plumbwell, Alex. Call him Mr. Plumbwell. Even here at home. And give him a chance. He only got started late last spring. He hasn't been here long."

"Do you know anything about him? Where did they find him?"

"Not under a rock. I heard you and Coker this morning. Mr. Plumbwell says he has family here. I think he intends staying around for a while, or he wouldn't have joined the museum board. Just be polite. You may end up liking him." She gave him a kiss and left the room.

A while later, he overheard her shouting to his hard-of-hearing Aunt Agnes who'd come by to borrow detergent. "Alex really doesn't like Harold Plumbwell. None of the kids do, apparently. I can't say I blame them. Something's wrong with that man. I caught a glimpse of his face after we found Mrs. Hamilton's body; I swear he was smirking."

"He's probably just one of those people who does inappropriate things when something ugly happens—you know, laughs nervously instead of crying."

"Laugh, smile? Maybe. But smirk?"

His mom was a nice lady, but why didn't she level with him like Ms. Mulholland did? He sighed a deep sigh. Moms are, like the saying goes, part of the problem, not the solution.

Usually Coker and Alex took the school bus, but the next morning Alex's mother drove them to school for early soccer practice. Alex was determined to become a star on the soccer field. Early soccer practice was vital. As they drove into the parking lot, Plumbwell came over to talk to his mother. Coker and Alex exchanged looks, and made a beeline for the field.

All day Plumbwell looked at him as if he was afraid of what Alex knew about him and Old Aggie. "Hey everybody, Plumber smirked when he saw Old Aggie's body. He did. With her bulgy eyes and her screaming mouth. My mom saw him. He smirked." Of course, Alex wouldn't say that. He could get kicked out of school. He did tell Coker who cracked up. "We should write a song about it," he guffawed. "We'll call it 'Bummer Plumber Smirked.' Four-four time with an upbeat. You do the lyrics, I'll do the music."

"Maybe." But Alex didn't mean it. Plumbwell scared him. Because the school was so small, almost quonset-hut-small, the principal's office was like a closet and he didn't stay in it much. Dressed in his same worn black suit every day, he wandered around, spying. He hid behind doors, waiting for someone to do something he could nail them for. His face was narrow and pinched, Alex and Coker thought from putting his nose places it didn't belong, as if it had been caught between too many doors and door frames.

The day went on and on, and the teachers kept piling on more homework. There was so much of it Alex knew he should do it instead of going to Old Aggie's house with Ms. Mulholland. But when he weighed priorities—that's what Ms. Mulholland said he should do—it was clear that murder was more important than class assignments of any kind. When the school bell rang, and the yellow Ford truck was there, waiting for him, he headed for it at a dead heat. Even at that, Plumbwell beat him. What now?

Alex climbed into the front seat. "I hope the little guy isn't having too much trouble dealing with Mrs. Hamilton's death,"

Plumbwell said, smiling at Ms. Mulholland on the driver's side of the truck.

"He seems to be doing well," she replied. It was annoying, both of them talking like he wasn't there. If only he could kick her. Him. Both of them.

"If there's any trauma, if there's anything we can do to help, please let us know."

"Thank you, Mr. Plumbwell. That's good of you." She started the motor, and he backed away. "Goodbye, now," she said.

"Goodbye, Ms. Mulholland. Goodbye, Alex." She gunned the motor, Plumbwell jumped.

"Well," she said, as they took off in a cloud of dust, "How are you, 'little guy?' Any trauma today?" They both laughed, and he felt better. In fact, he felt happy about his life for the first time all day.

On the way to Ms. Mulholland's, he told her what he overheard his mother say about Plumbwell, and what he found out about Mr. Crafts' real estate and the Major's painting. He could tell she thought his information was profound. He didn't pull out the picture of the painting for her to see right away, because she was driving and they were already at risk. At the house he handed it to her.

"I think it's the same painter as the one who did the Whittingtons' portraits. Nathan Howe. Doesn't that look like the same name?"

He couldn't make it out. His printer ink was running low

and it wasn't much of a copy. They went up to Ms. Mulholland's apartment to make sure Winky was okay—he'd been throwing up fur balls—and to put Alex's backpack away. Before they walked over to Mrs. Hamilton's house, Ms. Mulholland told him what she discovered hanging out with Director Dabney most of the day. They'd been doing an inventory and because it was such a dull thing to do, it was also a perfect time to get him to chatter.

Adrian remembered Crafts' affair with Aggie, but he was a very young man when it happened and he hadn't "given a fig." Wherever did he find that expression? Even though Aggie was good looking and rich when Adrian Dabney first came to the museum, she was much older than he was, and besides, she was especially nasty to him because the board had hired him to caretake the museum and he kept trying to do more than that. He'd wanted to organize the collections and preserve things, but it all cost money and she didn't want it spent that way. He'd started winning people over to his side because she made everybody hate her. After her accident, she was really addled—Alex's word for the day—and when he'd finally found enough votes to remove her from the board, she told him that she'd never forgive him and some day he'd regret it. He'd never taken the threat seriously.

"What accident?"

"She fell down some of the one hundred fifty-four stairs in the steeple of Boston's Old North Church. She thought she might get to play the bells."

"Paul Revere's church?"

"Indeed."

Adrian didn't know why Aggie asked everyone to come to the museum that morning, but he thought she'd been getting odder. She wanted to show them something "important for the future," and what she had to say was lengthy, he knew, because she'd told him it would probably take half an hour. He hoped it involved a sizeable donation. He'd asked the police to look in her pockets to see if she had notes for a talk, but they hadn't found anything. So maybe the killer took the notes. He didn't think she knew she was in danger, but she probably expected to argue with someone.

"Duh," murmured Alex.

"He tried to figure out what Aggie wanted to say from the people she'd invited, but he wasn't able to make sense of it."

VIII

The Hamilton House

Mrs. Hamilton's house stood on a stubby incline across the road, looking important. Painted pumpkin gold, it was two stories and square. The door was framed by Doric columns—it was amazing the things Alex knew that he hadn't known until last summer—and there was a fan-shaped window above it. According to Ms. Mulholland, it was a better example of the Federal-style than her house and had landmark status because it was one of the oldest buildings in town and used to be the post office where the stagecoach stopped. It was also rumored that the old jail was at the back of the house.

"I hope we can find a copy of Mrs. Hamilton's notes for Monday morning," said Ms. M. "Keep your eyes open."

It was hard to imagine the house without Mrs. Hamilton. One time, Coker had dared him to trick or treat her. That was the only time he'd ever walked up to the door, even though he'd seen her many times in the entryway, usually in her bathrobe, staring out at the steaming engines in the Antique Engines Show, or glaring at kids at summer camp while they played ball in the field across the road, but when he rang her bell at Halloween and she opened the door, he was afraid to say "Trick or Treat," or "Hello," because she was there, looking down at him, her eyes rolling in her round tomato face, and, worst of all, her bathrobe beginning to fall open. She looked all white and blubbery underneath, like the *National Geographic* picture he'd seen at the dentist's office of a puff fish. He'd had nightmares about Old Aggie for the next two months, dreams in which he'd end up in the jail below the house, its bars fronting nothing, just a dark earthen hallway and no people, because no one dared come and visit him. He pounded on the bars; he shouted curse words at her.

When he was seven he saw an *Antiquities* magazine with pictures of the inside of Aggie's house, so he knew that she might not look beautiful with her scroungy pink quilted bathrobe and her hair spread out like spider webs, but her house was beautiful, with shiny curlicued furniture and Oriental rugs, tapestries with unicorns, paintings of grim ancestors with gold frames, and drapes with silver and gold thread running through them. Since then, he'd overheard things. His mother and Ms. Mulholland worried about Old Aggie's decline, how her house was a fire hazard with boxes everywhere, and cobwebs hanging from the ceiling. He'd tried to re-imagine the pretty stuff with the boxes and cobwebs, but now he was going to see for himself.

The Hamilton House was especially exciting because Alex's

own house was a trailer and even though he had his own room, it was tiny. His mom was a "Walmartian," so, there was no mystery about where their furniture came from. A lot of people in Shrubsbury lived better than they did. Coker's family had a farmhouse with two bathrooms and a shingle roof. His room had slanting ceilings and looked out on the woods where he saw deer in the morning before school. Every winter he went hunting with his dad. Alex's father never came back to see him after he left, much less go hunting. The only thing Alex liked in the trailer was his computer and his posters from Rune Scape and the Animal Collective.

Ms. Mulholland knocked and Mrs. Hamilton's daughter swung the door open and stared down at Alex. Dressed in a not-quite-shocking purple kimono, with red hair to her waist and a big chin like Jay Leno, she reminded him of the redheaded witch in a book about English werewolves he'd found in the library. She didn't look like Mrs. Hamilton at all. Just as well. She fit the house better which, he was glad to see, still had paintings and tapestries. The furniture was dark wood, maybe mahogany, probably mahogany, but it was grayed over with dust. He couldn't see the rugs very well because there were so many boxes everywhere, but he did notice that they were scuzzy the way rugs got when no one was Hoovering them.

"I'm so glad you've come," said Serendipity Hamilton.

"Thank you, Sera. I haven't been in this house in a long time. Amazing how much more paper she found." Ms. Mulholland looked around at all the boxes.

"Newspapers, magazines, the library—yours and those from every town in the county. Come, I've made a fire and a space by it. We can sit and talk."

A card table and chairs had been pulled up in front of the fireplace. Alex had seen fireplaces before but nothing like this. It was painted cornflower blue with white willowy women carved on either side. And it came with a matching teapot and cups. Only the willowy women were missing from the cups.

Serendipity smiled at him with big white teeth. "Would you like a Coke, Alex?" His mother and Ms. Mulholland didn't approve of soft drinks, but Alex did and he saw an opening. "Is it okay?" he asked. Ms. M shrugged her shoulders and nodded.

"I'm afraid you're not the only ones to ask to look through all this paper," Sera Hamilton said, pouring the tea. "After the police, of course, Adrian came and went—I guess that makes sense. She always accused him of stealing from her; he thought she was the thief. I think he wanted to make certain there wasn't something here that should be in the museum. As far as I know he didn't find anything. More interesting, I have requests from a Major Lemuel Shelton, a Mr. Plumbwell, and a handsome fellow I've never met, Nick Crafts, who says my mother was his father's mistress."

"That's true, Sera. You knew she used to be quite beautiful."

"Terrifying, isn't it? If she could end up the way she did, what'll happen to me?" she called out as she went to the kitchen and opened the refrigerator to find Alex's Coke.

"As far as I know, you're neither demented or wicked, so chances are you'll age normally."

"Huh uh. You don't know me very well, Tasha." She came back to the table and poured out the Coke, then sat down and stared into her teacup. She looked like a gypsy reading tea leaves. Alex waited for a prophesy, maybe even a revelation about her mother's murderer. But it didn't come.

"Are you going to let the others in?" asked Ms. Mulholland.

"You know, I haven't decided. Maybe I'll make them wait until the will is read and we find out who the master or mistress of the house really is." Her gold hoop earrings flashed in the firelight. She nibbled on one of the small cakes she'd laid out for them. It had powdered sugar on top and for a moment her large red mouth was almost as white as her big teeth.

"Are you so certain that it's not going to be you?"

"I'll never forget the last time she growled that I was disinherited. I don't think it's going to be me."

"Why ever did she want to disinherit you?"

"Aside from the fact that she never liked me? I refused to marry and give birth. I wouldn't carry on the line. The line was more important than anything to her."

"Even her daughter."

"Yes. Oh, yes."

"I'm surprised she didn't try to have more children."

"I'm not certain she didn't. After meeting him, I wonder about Nick Crafts. And I've wondered, to be frank, about Lori Chickering."

"In the name of all that's holy, why Lori?"

"Because of the months, almost a year, that Lori could do no wrong. I was told that I should emulate her. Like all of my mother's relationships, it ended badly—she eventually hated her—but for a long time Lori might as well have been her daughter."

"Who would the father have been?"

"What about Adrian?"

"Sera Hamilton, I take back anything I've said about your sanity. You've gone loco."

"Do you really think so, Tasha? Think about Lori's face and tell me you don't see my mother and Adrian in it."

Ms. Mulholland and Alex stared into the fire, thinking about Lori's face. If it was true, Alex thought, pity poor Lori. Thank God, his mother was really his mother. What if Lori was some awful combination of Aggie and Adrian Dabney? Aggie's eyes, Adrian's mouth, Aggie's hair, Adrian's eyebrows...

Ms. M and Sera Hamilton finished their tea and turned their chairs around to stare at the scattering of boxes across the room. "Ms. Hamilton," Alex said tentatively, nervous that she'd stand up and loom over him and he'd lose the question. "Is there really a jail in this house?"

"That's the rumor, isn't it?" she answered him, and gazed into his face as if she were looking for the person who spread it, and it must, surely, be him.

"Yes, ma'am," he answered, his voice getting smaller.

"There is. I don't like to visit it. I haven't been down there at all since I got back. It's a nasty place littered with the bones of squirrels and rats. I was threatened with it my whole childhood."

So there would be no exploring the Hamilton House jail this visit, Alex noted. And he wouldn't dare ever ask again.

It turned out that Sera Hamilton knew what was in the boxes "generally," so the search wasn't as hard as Alex had feared. Even though it looked random, Aggie put things together that belonged together. She had a filing system. The collection in the living room was about antiques, and the black scrawl on each box described the articles inside: fainting couches, Windsor chairs, bird's-eye maple tables, fancy tall case clocks...

The kitchen was full of bottles of wine. "Did Mrs. Hamilton drink?" Alex asked, thinking that that would explain a lot. "No," said Sera Hamilton. "If she had, some of these bottles would be gone by now. Some of them date back to my childhood." She didn't try to hide several more recently emptied bottles of Absolut vodka in the trash can. On the chipped enamel cookstove there were stacks of scorched and grubby pots and pans. The counter and the sink were cluttered with crusted china: Aggie hadn't cleaned up after herself very well for a long time. "I'm sorry it's so awful in here, but I just can't bring myself to wash my mother's dishes. I really, really can't. Someone else, whoever gets it all, has to do it."

In the front parlor, they found boxes of papers about paint-ings and a round maple table with Aggie's computer, a china cup with a dried tea bag, and piles of printed information from the internet. The sheriff had taken a box of CDs and Aggie's hard drive but so far he hadn't found anything to help with the investigation, Ms. Mulholland reported. They looked for something about Nathan Howe and had almost given up when Ms. Mulholland mentioned the painter to Sera Hamilton, who pointed to the painting on the wall above the parlor piano. "Why didn't you say so? That's an 1837 Howe painting of this house. I grew up with it." While Sera Hamilton and Ms. Mulholland went upstairs, Alex squinted at the painting from different angles, hoping for another image to emerge, for a window to reveal Juliette looking out, or a bush by the porch, a baby carriage for Juliette's baby. He wondered if he'd have better luck at another time of day, when there was morning light.

Upstairs, in Mrs. Hamilton's bedroom, Alex went to the front window to look out on the Hinman Road, the very first road built in this part of Vermont. What did it look like from here when Juliette lived in this house? It wasn't a question he would have tackled normally, but he was trying not to look at Aggie's enormous featherbed with a rose-covered quilt so faded the color was more like a stain than a design and dingy yellowed sheets that Alex's mother would have washed long ago. Then, because he'd started looking and didn't know where else to look, he stared at the pink nightgown lying across the bed that still had her shape in it and the knotted up pillow with goose feathers oozing out. He didn't want to get anywhere near the bed or the side table with the glass of blue water where she kept her teeth overnight. He didn't want to get near enough even to read the title of the book beside the glass. Ms. Mulholland walked over and picked it up. *"Antiquities in New England,"* she read out loud. "By Abigail Shelton."

"The Major's wife!" Alex said, under his breath so Sera Hamilton wouldn't hear.

"And it's opened to paintings by Nathan Howe. May we borrow this, Sera?"

"I don't see why not. But I don't quite get what you're looking for, Tasha."

"Just Nathan Howe again. And genealogies."

Ms. M walked to the window to gaze with Alex at the late afternoon. Directly across the Hinman Road a wide strip of trees climbed up one side of a hill. They were beginning to turn red and gold. He liked the way the light looked when the sun was low and shooting across the earth instead of down onto it. He liked the way the woods gracefully wound their colorful way upwards, and he wondered whether Old Aggie had too, and how many times she'd looked out the same way he was. Probably thousands. Hundreds of thousands. For the first time he sort of liked her. He thought of the people before her, way back to Juliette Whittington. What had she been looking at when she looked out? A road. Where there were woods today, then there had been another road. Mrs. Hamilton's house had been at a crossroads. A different view, but the same.

"Ms. Mulholland, do you still have the picture from the website?"

"I think I kept it with me, Alex." She plunged her hands into her sweater pockets, and pulled it out. "What's on your mind?"

"Can I look at it?"

"Of course."

There it all was. The now absent road, the hill, but where trees and brush filled the scene today, there were sheep under a big tree, maybe a quarter mile up the road. Whoever Nathan Howe was, he'd painted the view from this window more than 165 years ago.

"You're talking about the old painting from this window, aren't you? Very clever of you to spot it with that bad copy, Alex, and with the trees and all," said Sera Hamilton. "I always thought it was overrated, but my mother loved it."

"She didn't own the painting, did she?" asked Ms. Mulholland.

"She did when I was growing up. Then she gave it to the museum. I guess it's not there anymore or you would know about it. I have no idea who owns it now."

"Thank you, Sera." Tasha Mulholland took the picture from Alex and put it back in her pocket. "If you remember anything else about it, I'd appreciate hearing."

"Of course."

Ms. Mulholland went through the drawers on Mrs. Hamilton's night table, still looking, Alex guessed, for the notes for her talk the day they found her body. There wasn't anything, just some cough drops and a used handkerchief. One of the boxes in the bedroom had old deeds and maps in it, and she collected some of those. "I hope you don't mind, Sera. I'll bring them back. They're interesting because I know we don't have them in the museum and we should at least have copies."

There were three more rooms upstairs. Sera was staying in her childhood bedroom. It was frilly and pink, girly, which, thought Alex, was to be expected even though Sera was hardly that now. There weren't any boxes in it, but Sera had a book about magic on her nightstand. The other bedrooms had been guest rooms but now they were stacked high with cutouts from old newspapers about gardening, Impressionist painting, and music boxes. None of them seemed important.

As Alex and Ms. M walked across the road back to her house, she thumbed through Abigail Shelton's book. The author's autograph on the flyleaf read, "To Agatha Hamilton who set the cradle rocking, Your new friend, Abigail." "What an odd autograph," she murmured as she showed it to Alex. "But touching somehow. And sad. Aggie was so hateful about her."

"Why ever would she have wanted to be friends with Mrs. Hamilton, Ms. M?"

Ms. Mulholland shook her head. "I can't imagine, Alex."

Alex was sitting in the kitchen waiting for his mother and reading aloud about Antarctica when he had a thought: "Ms. Mulholland," he said, interrupting himself. "I have a question."

"Yes, Alex?"

"Do you think Serendipity Hamilton is jealous of Lori?"

Ms. M was quiet for a minute, thinking about what he'd asked. "I'm not sure. She might be, I suppose. Why do you ask?"

"She sure made it seem like Lori might be the murderer. And another thing."

"Yes."

"Is there really a jail in the Hamilton House?"

Ms. M. shook her head. "I don't know, Alex. I really don't know."

"I wish I didn't have to go to school tomorrow."

IX

Principal Plumbwell at work

It was early the next morning. Principal Plumbwell was waiting on a bench for the soccer players to come up from the field. The teachers were inside, erasing the remains of yesterday's lessons from their blackboards and laying out newly crafted lessons for the day. Most of the children were on their way to their desks; the school bell would ring any minute, and Principal Plumbwell was practicing frowning and working his mouth into a mean scowl. The soccer players below had forgotten everything but the next kick, the next run, the ball. When they heard the bell, they'd come running. But some of them—from past experience, at the very least, Alex—would be late, and Plumbwell was waiting to stick it to them.

Plumbwell had discovered that a principal could really shake up the people around him, especially the kids. At first, he'd chafed at the idea that there was no space for an office in the school.

Shrubsbury had never needed one in the past. They'd done fine without a full-time principal and his office. Every day Plumbwell had to find somewhere to perch, or just wander from class to class like a warden in a prison, checking on teachers, students, and an occasional visiting parent. A man with few pleasures in life—driving, drinking, making a fast buck—he'd found one more: scaring the bejeezus out of people, especially people who had it in for him. Like Agatha Hamilton. Like the Churchill kid and the old lady the kid hung out with. An annoying old broad. Not someone he wanted anything to do with. But in his line of work there were always a lot of unimportant people to cater to.

He'd taken the job to monitor the dispersal of Agatha Hamilton's fortune. Now that the old witch was gone, he planned to make one last try for the money. Then he'd take off before anyone found out he wasn't who he seemed to be.

The one thing he'd learned in Shrubsbury was that he wasn't cut out to be a school principal. This had been Principal Plumbwell's first time out. The credentials and references had been easy to create—Harold was a master at making false documents. It was his one sure skill. His mother had been so impressed with his talents when he was a child, she'd sent him to art school where he'd perfected copying and counterfeiting and returned to save the family's hide more than once. "Principal" had been a way of getting to Shrubsbury and impressing himself on Mrs. Hamilton. The place wasn't exactly full of respectable jobs. And Aggie Hamilton had proved to be far more of a challenge than he'd expected. Usually a challenge was something to be enjoyed in his line of work. An easy con was no fun. But Shrubsbury was a pathetic excuse for a town. He'd promised himself Las Vegas when he finished here. Good riddance to Agatha Hamilton and Vermont.

The bell rang. The boys were clustered around the ball. One more opportunity to score. The goalie left his station and Alex couldn't help himself. This was his chance to put the ball in. He was the last one to come running.

"Okay, Alex. That's it. You're late again. All those minutes add up. You get no recess today."

"But we have a game tomorrow. I need to practice."

"The team will get along fine without you. You think you're important, but you're not. Math is what's important and that's what you'll do during recess today." He looked down at Alex, his face stern, his little eyes glinting and a slight curl to his lips.

He's enjoying this, thought Alex. The guy's a sadist.

X

Possible suspects

We haven't looked at three people who in most investigations would be suspects."

"Who?"

"You, your mother and me."

"Jeeze, Ms. Mulholland. I don't think I could have gotten Mrs. Hamilton into that churn. I guess my mom might have, but..."

Alex liked the idea of being a suspect.

"Well, there is that, and I think you have an alibi, don't you? Probably you and your mom?"

"Yeah, we didn't even get up until 7:00."

"What I'm thinking, Alex, is that Mrs. Hamilton may have had a reason for inviting you, and incidentally your mom, to come to the museum that morning. What do you know about your mother's past and her genealogy? Or your dad's for that matter?"

"Not much. You don't think we're related to Old Aggie?"

"It's highly unlikely, but see what you can find out, okay?"

"I sure hope we're not," he said, and shuddered. "What about you, Ms. Mulholland?"

"Yes. What about me? Why did she want me there? And incidentally, no, I'm not related and I don't have an alibi."

"It doesn't matter. You couldn't be a murderer. You're too cool."

"You think so?"

"And besides, you're an old lady."

"Old ladies make as good murderers as anyone else, Alex Churchill. You don't know all the times in my life when I've been so angry, I could have just... But it is true a knife wouldn't have been my weapon of choice. Something unlikely. Vegetable. Something that would rot away afterwards."

Sitting in front of the barn on a shimmering sun-filled afternoon, Ms. Mulholland spun—clackety whir, the wheel going round and round so fast it was a blur. Tourists stopped and watched. Just returned from Aggie's funeral, she had changed from funeral clothes to her old-time costume, a long blue and white flowered dress and a big blue bonnet. Because she was so tall she bent over the wheel, and from a distance it was as if she were a fairy tale character making magic, spinning gold from flax, thought Alex, reaching back into his not-so-distant past. During the summer, Alex put on a cap and pretended to be her old-time grandkid, but he felt silly wearing it, especially when women chucked him under the chin and strange men called him "son." While he and

Ms. Mulholland didn't look like detectives, they didn't look much like murder suspects either.

"So I'll try to find out things from my mom. What else? Did you learn anything at the funeral?"

"No. Everyone was there: Adrian and Lori, of course, the Major and his wife, Nick Crafts, Principal Plumbwell. Even your mother took a half hour from work. Sera looked extraordinary in mourning, and appropriately grim. Lori was the only person I saw with tears in her eyes. Everyone tried to be well-behaved and no one cheered."

"I wish my mom had let me go."

"You really didn't miss much, Alex. I hope I'll have more to report after the inquest tomorrow afternoon. Which, no, you shouldn't come to either. You're a kid. You can stay unobserved and that's where you should stay. You'll be able to find out much more that way."

"How?" he almost wailed. "How, when I'm not allowed to go anywhere?"

"Alex, Alex, Alex. Shush. There are things grown-ups do best and things kids do better. I've got a job for you. While the inquest is going on, I want you to search Lori Chickering's office. She's the kind of person who brings in home-cooked food and puts family pictures everywhere. She just might have something about her childhood in her office. And something about Mrs. Hamilton."

"What about Mr. Dabney?"

"I don't think you'll have time. Besides, he's a secretive man.

He's probably committed every secret he's ever had to memory. You're unlikely to find anything. The inquest will be short—give yourself no more than forty-five minutes. Get in and get out."

"You've got it!"

"While I'm at the inquest, I'll ask Major Shelton about the painting."

They watched as a car full of tourists with New York license plates passed by and pulled into the parking lot. "From the town clerk we know that there's no record of Juliette giving birth or of a baby dying. Nor is there any evidence that I can find that Agatha Hamilton gave birth to Nick Crafts, or Lori. No babies in the nineteenth century, or the twentieth. Maybe we're going about this the wrong way."

"It's a bummer. There must be something else I can do too. I mean besides the Lori thing."

"I've been thinking about that. You know I've talked to Lori and Adrian, and not learned much. I know they're not telling me everything they know. Why don't we see what you can get out of them this weekend? They'll both be working. Just hang around the gift shop. Lori will be there most of the time. Ask her about her childhood. Adrian plans to rake leaves—we couldn't get anyone to volunteer for the job. See if you can help him, and get him to tell you stories about Mrs. Hamilton while you work together. He has a million of them. What do you think?"

"Awesome. I'm on it." He didn't look forward to the hard labor or spending that much time with Dab who was a geek of colossal dimensions, but he'd watched enough TV drama to know that detectives have to be prepared to sit in cars with styrofoam cups of coffee for hours on end. This, he reasoned, was the Shrubsbury equivalent.

"Be very patient and subtle."

He was pleased to learn that what she meant by "subtle" was "sneaky."

They stopped talking about the murder when Principal Plumbwell drove up in his black Impala and leaned out the window. "Good afternoon, Alex, Ms. Mulholland," he said. "Any chance you can show me around the barn? Here I am on the board and I've never seen it."

"Of course," said Ms. Mulholland, ignoring Alex's jabs. "That's what I'm here for."

"You'll be sorry," said Alex as Plumbwell went to park his Impala, "He doesn't care about the barn, he's here for some nefarious reason." Nefarious. His word for the day, one that no one else at school would know.

"I hope you're right. We need him to do something nefarious, so we can figure him out."

Principal Plumbwell acted as if he'd never seen a plow or a snowroller or heard of sugaring, so Ms. Mulholland had to start at the beginning. Maybe he was from a big city somewhere, Alex speculated, and maybe he was born yesterday besides. She asked him about his family and he said he really didn't have any, his parents were dead, and he was divorced and never had children.

Where was the family Alex's mother said he'd claimed to have? Why had he really come here? To boring Vermont. He just needed to get away from it all. Sure, thought Alex, I'll bet!

"I had no idea sugaring was such a complicated topic. All the different spouts. The different colors and kinds of syrup. The weather."

"You must attend a sugaring party next spring, Harold."

"Sounds quaint. I hope I get to, but so far I'm not having much of a social life here."

"I'm sorry to hear that. It must be especially hard when, lo and behold, the one person you do know well is murdered."

"Aggie wasn't all that fond of me."

"I'm afraid that's true of most of us. Now, I want you to look over here at our dairy exhibit—our milking stool, our few decades old milking machine."

"Yes, I see. I can't imagine doing it though. Ugh. All those quivering udders. I think Aggie liked you, Tasha, didn't she?"

"No. Not really," she smiled at him. He contrived a smile back. "On this side where hay used to be stored," she continued, "you see our collection of farm machinery: plows, harrows, seeders, manure spreader, harvesters…"

"Even farming is complicated, I guess."

"And on the other side where cows were stabled, we have a sheep power and a horse power." She started to explain animal power when he interrupted her.

"And that mammoth round thing is—?"

"A snowroller."

"What happened to the snowplow?"

"It came later."

"You see how truly ignorant I am, Ms. Mulholland?"

"I'm afraid I do."

"I hope you're learning a lot here, Alex."

"Yessir."

"Thank you, Tasha. When I have more time, I'll stay longer and really learn something. It's difficult to be on the board of a museum when you haven't the faintest idea what it's all about."

"Why ever did you want to be on the board, Harold?"

"It was Mrs. Hamilton's idea."

"So you've known her for some time?"

"Yeah, from years ago down in Connecticut. We kept in touch. I looked her up when I came and she suggested some civic involvement, especially since I was going to be a principal here."

"Well, we're glad you're on the board. Any time you have a question, just let me know."

She was sooooo nice to him, it made Alex want to heave. She even took his hand and gave it a squeeze when he left. Alex put it straight to her: "He's not just a geek, he's worse. Why, why, why, why were you so nice to him?"

"For the same reason you're going to be. He wanted to know what we knew about him and we didn't know anything and we may not get to know anything unless he tells us."

"But now we know something about him besides his being

a really dumb flatlander?"

"I'm not sure about his intelligence. But I am pretty sure what he's been doing since he came to the museum. I think he was Mrs. Hamilton's spy on the board."

Even dressed in a silly costume, Ms. Mulholland was awesome. Of course. Old Aggie had never cared about anyone's civic involvement. Besides, she couldn't keep a friend for more than a few weeks. He wasn't her casual friend from years ago. But then who was he? And what's more... "Now that she's dead, why is he still hanging around? She doesn't need a spy anymore."

"I don't know, Alex. We've got another mystery on our hands, I'm afraid."

It was dinner time when Alex remembered that Ms. Mulholland never told him why she thought Old Aggie asked her to come to the museum that morning. She just told him she didn't have an alibi. Was she telling him that she might have murdered Aggie? He almost choked on the Kentucky Fried Chicken his mother had brought home.

"Are you okay, Alex?"

"Yeah. Just eating too fast." Of course, Ms. Mulholland couldn't have done it. She was a righteous lady, maybe the only one at the museum. But it was true that she had plenty of opportunity to commit the murder: she lived next door; she had keys to everywhere. She was strong for an old lady too. She moved furniture around all the time; she once arm-wrestled Alex to the ground. She might have been able to lift Old Aggie up and into the churn. If she couldn't do it by herself, she would have found someone to help her. Someone like Adrian Dabney. Yuk. Silly Dab. She wouldn't have asked him. She'd have asked Alex. He was her friend. Not Adrian Dabney. He was just weird.

No, Ms. Mulholland couldn't have done it. Not only was she a good person, she didn't have a motive. She didn't even hate Old Aggie the way everyone else did. And why would she have agreed to work with Alex on the case if she were guilty? Although it was true that trying to find the murderer made her look less suspicious. He hadn't suspected her at all until just now.

Alex had more trouble falling asleep that night than he'd had since Old Aggie died. It wasn't until the next morning that he wondered what had got into him the night before: he must have gone bonkers. Ms. Mulholland couldn't be the murderer. They were partners like Batman and Robin, Tom Sawyer and Huck Finn, Harry Potter and Hermione Granger.

Besides, no matter what she said, old ladies don't murder people.

XI

The Major and his lady

The inquest went about as Ms. Mulholland expected. The coroner found that the victim's throat was cut and that she died from a very considerable loss of blood. She'd been murdered by a person unknown, using a serrated bread knife. Sheriff Mulholland assured everyone that his office was following every lead and that the culprit would be discovered.

Afterwards, Ms. Mulholland caught up to Major Shelton and his wife. "Lem, I've wanted to talk to you. How are you? And you, Abigail? I'm so sorry your association with the museum had to turn so ugly. Are you okay?"

"Yes. Yes," the Major boomed, his tweed jacket puffing out as his broad chest expanded and his words turned louder. "It's been upsetting, I'll tell you. This kind of thing shouldn't happen in a town like Shrubsbury. Abigail's been having tremors and dizzy spells ever since." Tasha Mulholland found herself moved by the pale woman, still a girl really, her hair auburn, silky and beautifully placed, not like the less done up hair of most women in the Northeast Kingdom, her eyes huge, deep set and so violet they were nearly black in her small tight face. Clearly, she was frightened. "Dr. Goodsell prescribed something and she's doing better. Makes you wonder. The times we live in, terrible. Not surprising with all the violence on television; the sanctity of life is an idea that's down the tubes, I'm afraid. And the criminal class, my god how it's grown in the last few years. Just terrible."

"Yes, it is shocking, isn't it? You're right. Things like this don't happen here. I'm sorry you were so upset, Abigail. I hope you're feeling much better." Abigail Shelton smiled and nodded, and clung more tightly to her husband's arm as if his presence was all that kept her from paling to transparency, spilling to the ground, and disappearing in a mist.

"There's no discipline anywhere anymore. The children are lazy except when they're criminal." Lem Shelton continued. "I wouldn't be surprised if we discover that Mrs. Hamilton's murderer was a kid, one of those rappers probably, a bloodthirsty rapper, I'll bet."

"Yes. Well, it could be, I suppose." Tasha Mulholland made a quick turn with them to walk up the road toward their car, even though her truck was in the other direction. "I wanted to ask the two of you something. The funeral didn't seem the time or place for it, of course. Anyway, I was online the other day. I know, you might not expect that of me as old and old-fashioned as I am, but anyway, I was. At heart I'm a very young spirit. I was looking for

84

information about all the board members for a report that Adrian has to give to the state historical society and, lo and behold, I found you on eBay. I had no idea that the two of you were into antiquing. Also, I found your listing for a Nathan Howe painting. Howe painted some of our portraits in the museum, you know. A fine early American painter. Primitive painter. I would love to buy it from you. Is it very expensive?"

"My, my. It never occurred to me that you'd be interested in a Howe painting, Tasha. But of course, you're interested in many things," declared the Major. She could smell his after-shave; she could see his mustache bristle as he talked. He wasn't looking straight at her any more, his eyes were flitting from the town offices building they'd just left to a brown cow across the road to someone or something so far away he couldn't make it out. He didn't want to talk about Nathan Howe paintings. "Yes, it is a Howe painting. But if you saw it on eBay you must have noticed, we have bidders for it, more than one I'm proud to say. We're in the midst of a bidding war. Another seven days before bidding's closed. And the bids are high, much higher than we expected, aren't they, my dear?"

"They are high," Abigail managed to say, her thin frame wavering like a shallow planting by the car.

"Wherever did you find it?" asked Tasha Mulholland.

"You know, I'm not sure I remember? Do you, Abby? We've had it for quite some time now."

"No, Lem. Not that long. I think one of your friends brought it to us. I can't remember when."

"We had better be on our way, Tasha. You can see that my wife's still not well. I want to get her back to the house before she faints dead away right here on the road."

"Yes, yes, of course," said Tasha Mulholland, watching as Mrs. Shelton helplessly tried to protest her good health. "I'll go look at the site again then and see if I can afford to bid." The Sheltons were already in their car. The Major lowered the window. "Good, good. See you soon then. We'll talk more about paintings. We have others. Maybe there's something else you'll want." He started the car, and was off, down the road, relieved, she supposed, to have gotten away from the nosy Ms. Mulholland.

XII

Being a detective takes some getting used to

B ack at the Old Shrubsbury School Museum, Ms. Mulholland found Alex dutifully pulling a rake across the grass, piling up leaves, while Adrian Dabney, leaning on his rake like it was a podium, recounted his years at the museum, remembering, it seemed to Alex, every object acquired, its provenance and its history, all in encyclopedic detail. "I remember the excitement when we received Elijah Cleveland's box of cobbler's tools, and along with it a framed certificate he'd won at the New England Industrial Fair of 1832 for the shoe polish he'd invented. He was a grand old man. You remember his picture, Alex—the whiskered fellow in the Coventry Room. His daughter—can you believe it—his daughter gave it all to us. She was the daughter of his old age, and her daughter still lives in the house Elijah built those many years ago. The Black River flows by it; the remains of an old mill are still in back of the house.

"We keep the past alive here—memories, Alex, memories. They give an extra dimension to reality. The present is wider and higher; everything has more resonance; the new has deep roots and its meaning is written in volumes not just a few panels in a comic book."

"I'd like to borrow Alex, if I may, Adrian," interrupted Tasha Mulholland. "I need someone to help me move a cabinet upstairs."

"Of course, Tasha. Though he is the most marvelous assistant. Come back when you're finished, Alex. I want you to understand why your work here is so important."

Alex followed Ms. Mulholland like an obedient puppy across the lawn to her house. "Has he been awful, Alex?"

"He makes school seem like Disneyland."

"Remember it's all for a good cause. Disneyland wouldn't have been. I gather you haven't been able to steer him to the topic of Aggie and her murder. Maybe we can figure out a way to move him along. Did you have any luck in Lori's office?"

"I think so. I found some pictures, but I haven't had a chance to really study them. I don't know whether they'll amount to anything."

"Let's go upstairs and have some cocoa. We'll look at them together."

Sitting in the kitchen, stroking Winky, Alex waited patiently while Ms. Mulholland changed back into her work clothes, and boiled up some cocoa. "Did you learn anything at the inquest?" he asked, only slowly coming around as his senses, dulled by Adrian's chatter, began to revive.

"It was very pedestrian, most of it. Nothing we don't already know. But, I did talk to the Major about the painting. and I'm afraid my ignorance almost betrayed me."

"How's that?"

"I don't know a thing about eBay, Alex. You've got to educate me about the internet. I must have sounded so stupid to the Major. I didn't know that people bid on eBay. It was hard to tell what he made of me, I hope just a dithery old lady. Anyway, it was clear he didn't want to talk about the painting, and he didn't want his wife to say anything either. Especially about where they got it. Can we find out who's bidding and how much?"

"We won't be able to find out who, but we can find out how much."

"Well, that'll be something, I guess." She gave him a big purple mug of hot chocolate and herself a smaller red one, and sat down across from him. He emptied an envelope full of pictures onto the table. A few were current; some were old snapshots, a few were computer printouts. "I hope she won't miss these," Ms. Mulholland murmured. "I don't know if you should have taken them."

"She'll never miss them—she's a mess. I don't know how she finds anything. She's for sure got the same genes as Mrs. Hamilton. Besides, the pictures were in a little inside drawer, a secret drawer."

"How did you know where to find a secret drawer?"

"It's like your desk."

"Amazing. I didn't know you knew about that drawer, Alex,"

she said uneasily, reviewing the contents of her secret drawer, and wondering if she should be angry. Since Adrian had talked the poor boy into a major funk, she decided not. "Were Lori's pictures all together when you found them?"

"Yes, and in the envelope. It has her name on the front; I think that's Old Aggie's handwriting."

"Mrs. Hamilton, Alex. Mrs. Hamilton's handwriting. I think you're right. So then the question is, did she give these to Lori, or did Lori collect them and try to give them to her? The first option is the most likely." She sipped at her chocolate for a full minute. "We're going to go back to Adrian and help him rake some more."

"Bummer," Alex muttered.

"It's okay, Alex," she laughed, gently because she felt sorry. "There's only a bit more on the other side of the building. The proximity to the root cellar might unnerve him, especially if he's guilty. We want to ask him how he found Lori, what he knows about her, who he thinks she is. I'm pretty certain he's going to lie. We'll try to catch the lies."

"How can we tell if someone lies?"

"How can we tell if Adrian lies? Everyone's different."

"I'm not sure with Dab. He's shifty-eyed most of the time. He never looks me in the eye. It's like he thinks I think he's lying."

"Yes. Exactly, Alex." Alex was remarkable, she thought. "I believe—I may be wrong—that most of the time he's in lying mode. He might as well be lying because he feels like he's lying. Adrian doesn't feel secure about who he is, so he always wants to reassure everyone around him that he's okay. Just an ordinary man."

"So most of the time he's acting, and he's a really bad actor."

"Yes."

"That makes it even harder to tell when he's really lying, doesn't it?"

"Not necessarily. There are levels. When he really is lying he begins to twitch. He drums his fingers as if he were a piano player, which he isn't. He tries to laugh—"

"And he can't stop smiling."

"Indeed." She began to shuffle through Lori's photos. Most of them were unimportant pictures of the museum and the grounds. There were also two fading snapshots of a baby, probably Lori herself. There was another with Lori, the little girl, and a couple who must have been her parents. Finally, there was a picture of a woman in her late thirties or early forties, a chubby woman, or more likely a pregnant one with a man who'd turned away from the photographer, but who looked familiar. Very familiar.

"Nick Crafts' father?" asked Alex.

"No. He's too thin to be Nick Crafts' father. Crafts was a bulky man. But the woman is Aggie Hamilton."

"That's Old Aggie?" Alex studied the photograph in amazement.

"That's her. She was still pretty then, wasn't she?"

"Yeah. She looks like a normal person. Weird. So maybe that means Lori is Mrs. Hamilton's daughter and that's her father?"

"It looks like someone thought so. Whether that someone

91

was Lori or Aggie, we don't know." She put a thumb on either side of the man for a moment. "That could be Adrian, you know."

"Eerie," he squinted at the picture. "I can't tell with his back to us."

Tasha Mulholland slid the pictures back into their envelope and tucked them into a pocket in her cardigan. "We'll make copies downstairs on our way out," she said.

"Lori's a really good suspect, isn't she? I mean she's strong. She was the one who wanted to know all about the butter churn, but not the root cellar. I bet she tried to talk Mrs. Hamilton into believing she was her daughter, and when Old Aggie didn't believe her, she killed her."

"Maybe. I suppose it's possible. Let's talk to Adrian, and then we'll go chat with Lori for a while."

Alex shuddered. "She's always seemed like a regular person. I mean her laugh is unreal, but... When you look at someone and you think they might have cut an old lady's throat—that's wicked."

"Yes. Are you okay, Alex? Can we do this or will it bother you too much?"

"I'm okay. Being a detective just takes some getting used to."

"It sure does," Ms. Mulholland agreed. It wasn't easy for an old lady either, to imagine Lori Chickering cutting Aggie's throat. On first acquaintance, and most people never got past that, Lori was exceptionally average. She wasn't especially attractive—she was lanky and her face was too long. Nevertheless, she did look a little like the young Aggie—her eyes and her smile were reminiscent of Agatha Hamilton's—but it was Aggie gone wrong. The length of her face put her eyes too far from her mouth, which was oversized but thin-lipped. Her nose didn't fill the space adequately. Nonetheless, she had beautiful eyes—dark, penetrating eyes like Agatha Hamilton's before they turned rheumy. Her youth made people think she was just another young woman. But her eyes gave the lie to her mouth: they were always serious. Lori thought a lot. Ms. M wondered about what.

They walked back to the museum to find Adrian Dabney still at work. "If it's too distressing for you folks to be here, I don't mind doing this myself."

"We've got to get back to normal, don't we?" said Ms. Mulholland, taking a rake in hand and giving Alex another.

"We do indeed. Did you learn anything at the inquest, Tasha?"

"Not a thing. Nothing new there, I'm afraid." She began raking vigorously. "Why didn't you go, Adrian? Everyone who was in the kitchen that morning was there. Except for Alex and his mother. And you."

"I let Lori represent me. She really wanted to go. I didn't. Too gory for my taste."

"Lori's an interesting girl. Where did she come from again?"

"Connecticut. I think Mystic Seaport. At least she worked in the museum there before she came here."

"It's a good museum, isn't it? A lot bigger than ours. Why would she exchange a job there for one at our poor little shop?"

"I don't know. I really don't. Of course, once she came she found a boyfriend." He began to get twitchy.

"She and Nick make a lovely couple, I think. I keep hoping for a wedding on the lawn."

"Yes. That's the way it seemed at first. Hard to say now. I think she's here because she likes being a big fish in a small pond. Mystic has a large staff. She might not have had much responsibility there for years."

"She's made lots of friends here," said Alex. "She was even Mrs. Hamilton's friend for a while."

Adrian laughed uneasily. "Yes, she was. Ms. M and Lori, and I guess Nick, were the only people to get along with Aggie for almost as long as I can remember." He put on an ironic smile, and raked with greater care, as if there were something besides leaves to pick up, something precious and delicate.

"What happened with Lori and Aggie to end it?"

"Aggie didn't like Lori's affair with Nick. She made sure it ended and ended quickly. Lori fought back."

"But she seems to still care about Mrs. Hamilton. Almost as if Aggie were her mother. What about her own family? Doesn't she have relatives in Connecticut?"

"Yes. She goes home for Christmas every year. She went back last spring when her father—I guess he was her stepfather—died."

"I had no idea. The poor girl. She never said a thing to me about it."

"Nor to me. Just the bare facts. I don't think they're a very close family." Adrian was very uncomfortable now, smiling broadly, rocking back and forth from one foot to the other. She could see him looking for a courteous exit. He had things he must do, and soon.

"She's been a good worker. We're lucky to have her."

"Absolutely."

"I think, especially at times like this, we should support each other. The other day must have been dreadful for Lori. As soon as we can clear some time, Adrian, maybe when we close the museum down for the winter, you and Lori will come to dinner. I'll do my meatloaf—you've always loved it. By then we should all be ready to talk about poor Agatha again. Your relationship with her was certainly a long difficult one."

"Yes." He was sweating.

"By then we should know who the monster was who killed her."

Adrian flashed his falsest smile. "Tasha, I'm going to let you and Alex finish. I do have things to do. Don't be too particular."

"No problem, Adrian." He left hurriedly, as if he heard a telephone ringing, as if someone somewhere were yelling for him, as if he had to find a bathroom before he got sick.

"We sure got him upset, Ms. Mulholland."

"We certainly did," she replied, "but I'm not sure about what." They worked quietly, both of them trying not to look at the door to the root cellar. "Of all the other people who might have had a key to the root cellar, Aggie was the most likely. Especially since she borrowed my key ring a few weeks ago. She gave it right back, but I wouldn't have noticed if the root cellar key wasn't on the ring for a day or so. She could have had one made, then somehow replaced it. You know, we should go to the hardware store and see if they remember her asking to make a copy of a key about that time. One thing about Aggie—she was always memorable."

"But we still haven't any idea what she wanted to do in the root cellar."

"I know. I'm going to ask Stuart if we can go in and look again one of these days."

On their way over to Lori's office, Ms. Mulholland suggested they try a shock tactic.

"Shock tactic?"

"Yes. I'm going to return Lori's pictures to her."

"Oh, man. You're not going to tell her I took them, are you?"

"Oh, no. I'm going to tell her I found them, and let her worry about who did."

"Awesome," Alex said. "Absolutely awesome."

Lori greeted them merrily when they knocked at her open office door. "What did you think of the inquest, Ms. Mulholland?"

"I thought it wasn't very informative. How about you?"

"Same."

"We came by mostly because Alex wondered if there was anything that you needed done tomorrow. He helped Adrian rake leaves today. Do you have any better jobs?"

"I don't like raking either, Alex. But I'm not sure that filing is more fun. I do need some of that done."

Alex shrugged. "I'll help," he said, wondering why a detective's work had to be quite so irksome.

"Great," Ms. Mulholland said. "The other thing. I found this envelope upstairs in the museum. Your name is on it, so I guess it belongs to you."

"Yes. Yes, it does." Lori's flushed face turned redder as she took the envelope. "I don't understand how it got there. I guess I should do a better job of hanging onto my things," she said, slowly recovering from her first surprise. "It looks like my messy office is traveling now," she smiled.

"Yes. I guess that can happen, our litter spreads out. I did take the liberty of looking inside, Lori. I'm sorry. You must know by now that I'm a very nosy sort of person, and don't always do what's expected of me. I saw your name on the front and I shouldn't have looked inside, but when I saw there were pictures I couldn't help myself." Lori put the photographs in her upper right hand drawer, trying to appear casual about what was clearly anything but.

"The photo with the couple. Is that Mrs. Hamilton? It's hard to believe, isn't it? She was really quite lovely. How many years ago was it taken? Who's the gentleman with her?"

"Yes, it is Agatha Hamilton. I don't know how many years ago, and I'm not certain who the fellow is. When Aggie and I were friends—it seems like an eternity ago—she loaned it to me along with all those pictures of what the museum used to look like. I stuck some old shots of myself my mom found in our attic at home in the same envelope, and forgot about them. Thank you for retrieving them, Tasha."

"You're more than welcome, Lori. How are you doing? I know Agatha's murder must have been awful for you. You knew her better than most of us."

"She was a very strange woman. I can't believe she's really dead."

"Hmmmmm."

"I'd hoped for a reconciliation with her but it's too late now." She sighed.

"Why did she turn on you, Lori?"

Lori looked confused for a minute. "I'm sorry, Tasha. Thinking about Aggie is very hard for me just now. And I do have to get home. I have a dinner date."

"I hope you and Nick have a good time—he's very handsome. You go along. And I'm sorry if I intruded, dear."

"No, no. It's okay. I'll see you tomorrow, Alex."

"Yeah," said Alex, raising his eyebrows at Ms. Mulholland— how had she known Lori was going out with Nick? "Tomorrow."

XIII

Alex at home

On Saturday night, Coker and Alex played their first soccer game of the season, and lost. Alex was feeling bad when he sat down at his computer after dinner. All he could think about was the clear shot he hadn't taken. It was going to be harder not to be a nerd than he'd thought.

As painful as it was, his future as a nerd was easier to worry about than Old Aggie's murder where everyone looked guilty, even though there was no evidence against them. He was confused, much more confused than any of the detectives on TV who always had suspects and evidence besides. He didn't have any better shot at being a detective than a soccer player. He played SimCity until he got bored. He found his mother in the living room darning socks and watching a CSI rerun. Gil Grissom was thinking and looking at something in a microscope.

"Do you think Sheriff Mulholland has a microscope?" he asked, slumping into his favorite easy chair, the one with the

99

stuffing beginning to show at the bottom and nothing to do about it except go back to Wal-Mart.

"I doubt it, Alex. He's not doing forensics. I think he has to send the evidence somewhere, maybe to Montpelier."

"How do you know stuff like that, Mom?"

"Old age, probably. What's wrong, Alex? It's only the first game. The season is just beginning."

"I know. But I was a real screw up."

"You were as good as everyone else on your team. Well, maybe not Joe. But oh, I'd hate to have a son like Joe. Soccer is all he's good at."

"Thanks, Mom." His sloppy mom with her pink pedal pushers and "Mother of an Honor Student" tee shirt knew just what to say. Her face was pretty in the lamp light, and she was right. Joe was a jerk.

Watching Gil Grissom solve the crime, he thought again how easy it looked. All that equipment. If only they had even a little bit of it. Maybe he should sit and outline his and Ms. M's case before bed. Grissom did a lot of that kind of thinking. It was going to have to be brains that solved it, not fingerprints or DNA or the rate at which ants eat the human body. He suddenly remembered he was supposed to find out about his genealogy. "Mom, we're not related to Mrs. Hamilton, are we?"

"What? Are you hoping she left you something in her will? It's very unlikely we're related. On my side, your grandmother was a German immigrant and your granddad's from England. They came to Vermont sometime in the middle 1800s. Your father's family goes way back in this part of the world, but if there's any relation I think it must be very distant. As much as Aggie talked about the Hamilton ancestral tree, I don't remember her mentioning any Howes. You met Grandma Howe years ago when you were just a toddler. I don't know if you remember her. She's a nasty piece of work, but she knows about your dad's ancestry. She still lives over in North Troy. If you wanted to ask her anything you could call. She might give you an answer. Why do you want to know?"

"'Cause Ms. Mulholland and I have been working on genealogies."

"If you and she ever really do work on our genealogy, let me know. I'd be curious."

"I will, Mom. Goodnight," He gave her a kiss on the cheek, feeling clumsy about it as he did. He almost never kissed her anymore since he'd gotten older and didn't do mushy stuff. Another question came to him. "Why aren't we Howes if my dad was?"

"I was very angry when your dad left. I was so angry I wanted to forget he ever existed. Try not to ever get that angry, Alex. It's a terrible way to be. Anyway, I changed my name back to Churchill, and changed yours too."

Alex nodded. "Churchill is good. Goodnight again, Mom."

"Goodnight, Alex. You're my guy. Don't ever forget it."

Sitting up in bed in his Batman pajamas, he wrote down his ideas from the day. First of all, Howe. Like the painter. It wasn't an unusual name. It probably didn't mean anything, but you never knew, and he could hardly wait to tell Ms. M.

He remembered that Mr. Dabney wasn't comfortable talking about Lori, and especially about her stepfather. Lori pretended not to know who the fellow in the photo with the young Aggie was. Ms. Mulholland was probably right, that it was Mr. Dabney. So was Lori the daughter of Aggie and Adrian Dabney? Or did she just pretend to be to get Aggie's money? How could Aggie and Mr. Dabney have possibly made a baby together when they hated each other so much? Tomorrow, while he filed, he'd talk to Lori about being a kid. He just had to figure out how to get her to talk. If only he were a cop and could haul her into the station and do good cop, bad cop with Ms. Mulholland. She'd be good, he'd be bad.

XIV

Alex gets subtle

I s it pretty in Connecticut?" Alex asked, as he began to rifle through some of Lori's random stacks of brochures and ads about everything: cleaning old stoves, repairing butter churns, and, would you believe, restoring old underwear.

"I guess," she said, as if she hadn't quite heard him or maybe needed time to think about the answer. "It is. But not as pretty as here."

"But more interesting, I'll bet."

"What kind of interesting are you looking for?"

"I dunno. Famous people, scary crimes, those kinds of interesting."

"Well, maybe yes, then. But we never found a body in a butter churn there."

"I guess you liked Mrs. Hamilton, huh?"

"Kind of. Sometimes very much."

Not sure he had the patience to wait for her to say something interesting, Alex decided to plunge in and take a chance. "Mrs. Hamilton's daughter said her mother used to treat you like a daughter."

"Sera said that?"

Alex nodded slowly, solemnly.

"Well, she did for a while. Then she decided I wasn't what she wanted in a daughter."

"Was she really nice to you when you were her daughter?"

"When I was her sort of daughter."

"So how did she act nice?"

"She gave me compliments and presents, stuff like that."

"And she didn't yell at you?"

"Not as much as she did everybody else." Lori grinned.. The interview was vaguely amusing.

"Did you want her to be your mother?"

"Yes, very much, I did, Alex. Now get back to work. I have to concentrate on what I'm doing."

For five minutes Alex filed papers while Lori wrote letters on museum stationery. "I think she'd have been a really lousy mother," he said. "Didn't you have your own mother?"

Lori stopped typing. "My mother and father adopted me when I was a baby. I didn't like them very much. My mother wasn't like yours. She was mean and selfish. Aggie may have been screwy, but when she liked you, she was warm and lavished you with affection. Now, since you volunteered for this job, I suggest you get down to work."

The thought of being lavished with affection by Aggie made Alex wince. Each to his own. Takes all kinds. But weird. Really weird. But since he'd annoyed her already, he might get away with one more question. He was only twelve; she'd have to forgive him.

"She was very rich. I guess she lavished you with money too."

"Alex!!" Lori almost yelled, her face as red as the sweater she wore. "You are the most discourteous boy this morning. So what if she was rich, you little reprobate. It's none of your business."

She didn't have a cool bone in her body. He'd struck a nerve. He didn't want her to see the smile on his face. He bent down close to the file he was working on; he'd probably done as much as he could today. He'd have to ask Ms. Mulholland what a reprobate was.

XV

Ms. Mulholland sees an attorney

As it turned out, Ms. Mulholland didn't need Sera's invitation to the reading of a will. Rupert Young, Esq. explained on the telephone that there would be no reading, that it had been postponed until certain conditions were met. Mrs. Hamilton's last will and testament "was not usual." Since Aggie had appointed Tasha Mulholland her executrix, he needed to talk with her at once.

Tasha knew Rupert Young, Esq. only slightly from museum events. Aggie introduced him at a fund-raiser as her family's long-time legal representative. Tasha remembered he looked like a lawyer retained by a wealthy family should look, at least in a PBS adaptation of an English novel. Trim in a double-breasted suit made of the best worsted, his shoes were black Italian leather and shiny, his glasses were rimless, his gray mustache was pencil thin and his silvery hair was beautifully puffed and coiffed. The time had been too brief to penetrate his disguise and his cologne and find the man, whoever he might be. Now, in his office, she realized that the reason she hadn't figured him out was that she couldn't see his eyes. Behind the spectacles they were a nondescript washed-out color. If they hadn't been framed by the glasses and his dark arched eyebrows, they might have disappeared altogether. His jaw and cheeks had been plucked clean of any stray whiskers and the skin stretched like a plastic sheath over the delicate bones of his face. When she'd first met him, he'd been stiff and distant. He'd almost extended his arms to keep her at arm's length; he'd continued to call her Mrs. Mulholland even after she'd instructed him to call her by her first name. Now, in his office, he was no more familiar, speaking in a sonorous voice that sounded rehearsed but probably wasn't. After all, what kind of person could memorize perhaps a half hour's worth of remarks and sentiments and then perform them for an audience of one? And without the context of a play?

"Please sit down, Mrs. Mulholland. I've taken the liberty of ordering us some tea, some Earl Grey as a matter of fact, since it seems to be the universal favorite. I hope that's satisfactory." She sat down as he began to pour. "Please help yourself to cream and sugar." He took his place opposite her behind a maple desk that was so massive, she hoped they'd be able to hear each other across its expanse. Above it and behind him was a large painting of a gentleman with mutton chops who looked uncannily like the occupant of the desk. The past as presentiment of the present.

"Mrs. Hamilton, as you know, was quite an eccentric, and

I'm afraid her will is just as oddly made as she. It assigns you an unusual and not very pleasant task."

"She never asked me if I would be willing to be her executrix. Did she name someone else to do the job if I refuse?" Ms. Mulholland knew she must sound petulant; in fact, she was probably angry.

"I told her she must ask you. Apparently, she was afraid you'd say no. I insisted she find someone to take your place if that became necessary. She settled on her first husband who, as it turns out, is senile. I think she may have got the best of us. Let me describe the task. It may not be as arduous to you as I made out."

Tasha Mulholland sipped her tea and settled back in her chair to listen.

"Mrs. Hamilton had been advised by her doctor that she might not have much time left. That's why she'd been consulting with me for the last month or two. She wanted all of her property and her monetary wealth to go to a legitimate heir or heirs. What she asks of you is that you determine the identity of that person or persons. It seems that about thirty years ago Mrs. Hamilton gave birth to a baby immediately after an accident in which she was critically injured. Her husband at the time, I believe he was the second, who may or may not have been the father, gave the baby up for adoption. By the time Mrs. Hamilton had recovered sufficiently to ask questions, the baby was gone and so was her husband. He died not long after. Relieved at the time that the child was no longer her responsibility, Mrs. Hamilton did nothing to try to find the infant. Only later when her daughter Sera declared she would not give Mrs. Hamilton a grandchild and heir to her fortune, did she worry about the other infant. If that poor misbegotten child can be found, she or he will inherit everything.

"To make matters more difficult for you, Mrs. Hamilton came up with an alternative. For most of her life, she believed that her ancestor Audrey West, who was the daughter of the original inhabitant of Mrs. Hamilton's house, was the only one of two daughters to bear children. There's a straight line from Audrey to Mrs. Hamilton. Juliette, Audrey's sister, was said to have been barren and died young. Recently, Mrs. Hamilton discovered that at least one genealogy shows that Juliette was the mother of a girl. Whether that genealogy is to be believed, whether the child died in childbirth or at an early age, or lived into adulthood, isn't known. But there is at least a chance that she lived and had progeny of her own and that there are descendents somewhere, Mrs. Hamilton's distant cousins. If her own child cannot be found, she would like to see her property and money go to that descendent or descendents. There are guidelines as to how the inheritance should be divided if both the child and descendents are found.

"If no heir is uncovered within a month's time, if the Hamilton line can't be continued, Mrs. Hamilton is willing that it all be passed on to her daughter Sera."

"Quite a challenge, Mr. Young. I assume she'd been trying to find these missing relations. Why should I have any better luck than she did?"

"You may not, but she was working on the project up until

109

her death. She felt that she was very close to success. Since she had a presentiment that her death was imminent, the will is very recent, and about two weeks ago she left some papers with me. I would like to hand that information over to you."

"She's made me a target for the same person who murdered her, you know. Not the kindest thing to do to a friend."

"You have the advantage of secrecy. I've told no one about Mrs. Hamilton's assignment to you. I've told anyone who asks that the reading of the will must be put off for a month because of its particulars, but I've given nothing away."

"Shrubsbury is a place where secrets lose traction almost before they're formulated."

"If you feel you have reason to be afraid, perhaps you can get special protection. I understand Sheriff Stuart Mulholland is your son."

"Oh, my," murmured Tasha. "What a terrible thought." Since she had no idea what to say next, it was just as well that Rupert Young's secretary buzzed him with an important telephone call. Excusing himself, he stretched over his wide desk to clasp her hand in a quick, cold, muscular grip. Feeling more dithery than usual, she was about to leave when he barked, "The envelope, Ms. Mulholland. Remember your envelope." He reached out toward her again, this time with the envelope in his hand. She hesitated for only a moment, took it and left.

Tasha Mulholland gunned the motor and barreled down the

highway and onto the road that led back to Shrubsbury. Usually, passing through the town that bordered it, she looked to see who was at the hardware store or the bank. She'd planned to stop and borrow a book at the library. Instead, she drove past it over the speed limit, her eyes fastened on the road ahead. She didn't wave when she passed Lori on an afternoon jog. She saw her, but the girl seemed entirely different to her now, threatening, even sinister.

She'd intended to buy coffee at the quick stop and take the hike from the bridge down to the Willoughby River where the water was rough and cascaded through the rocks. Drinking coffee by white water had always been one of her favorite pastimes. But her life had been turned upside down and she didn't know whether contemplation would be possible. She'd already gone by the quick stop when she pulled the truck to the side of the road, and glared at nothing in particular. She'd be damned if she'd let a pasteboard lawyer and a mentally ill old woman, not even alive, for God's sake, keep her from coffee and white water. She turned the truck around and went back for the coffee.

Making her way down to the river, she was herself again. She was graceful on the rocks the way she never was when people were around, feeling the spray on her face like a baptism, searching out her rock, the one shaped like a mermaid's throne, letting the rumble and roll of the water take her and hold her apart from the world and its meanness.

Lost in the white silence inside the roar of the water, she didn't immediately see Sera Hamilton standing over her, or hear her calling. "Hello, Tasha." Her red hair streamed around her, her eyes were huge and bright. "May I join you?"

What was she to say? She wanted her gone, but Tasha Mulholland had been raised to be courteous. In fact, that's what had gotten her into the trouble she was in now. Graciousness to the older Hamilton. How could she be anything but the same to the younger one? "Of course, Sera."

For a few minutes they sat silently, not trying to compete with the water, just letting it have its way, filling the space between them. But of course they couldn't do that indefinitely. "I saw you at Rupert Young's office. I followed you. That's why I'm here," Sera called out.

"I see," said Tasha Mulholland.

"Are you my mother's executrix?" Serendipity Hamilton demanded and her face began to blow up the way Aggie's sometimes did—big, flushed, pulsing with anger the way a volcanic site must pulse with heat just before the eruptions begin. "Did she enlist you to dispose of me?" the woman shouted at her.

"That's what she may have intended," Tasha Mulholland replied as loudly as she could, trying to keep her voice contained like liquid in a bottle. "I can't talk about this now, Sera. I don't know what I'm doing. Not yet."

"Let me tell you what you must not do," hissed Sera Hamilton in her ear. "I've suffered every indignity, every deprivation at my mother's hands. You must not let that go unrecompensed. You must not leave me out here after all these years, not just unavenged but unredeemed. It's my inheritance. If you do anything to take it away from me, you'll be sorry. I didn't kill my mother but I could have. I'm entirely capable of murder." She stood up and stared down, looking suddenly like something horrible, something Tasha remembered seeing. Serendipity Hamilton's face was like Aggie's face in the butter churn. Angry. Terrified. A face that turned her stomach and left her reeling.

XVI

Ms. Mulholland turns chicken shit

Tasha Mulholland locked the downstairs door to the Cyril Benning House, something she'd never done, not even when there had been burglaries in the neighborhood five years earlier. She made herself a cup of exceptionally strong black coffee and paced the floor. Her shock at finding herself frightened was worse even than being afraid. She realized that until now she'd shut out the horror of Aggie's death. She'd never liked the woman, and it was a fact that, as Sera said, the death was fitting. But it had been grotesque and worse, pathetic, pitiable. If the murderer was capable of that, might he, or she, be happy to do something gruesome to another old lady? She wasn't in the least ready for any of this. She should have stalked back into Rupert Young's office, returned his envelope, and told him to go hang.

But, of course, she couldn't help wanting to know what was in the envelope, so without really thinking about it, she opened it. Inside was a copy of a birth certificate for a baby, Lori, born to Agatha Hamilton, and a copy of a letter from Aggie to Lori nearly thirty years later accusing her of falsifying the document and, with her supposed father, Adrian, trying to con her supposed mother, Agatha. There was a picture of the elder Crafts with an infant whose sex was uncertain and a second picture of Crafts Sr. with a pregnant Aggie.

The most curious item was a genealogy showing descendents of Juliette and Gerald Whittington, and their daughter, Isabelle. Among those descendents, in fact the only one now living, was Principal Harold Plumbwell. It wasn't clear who made the genealogy, but Tasha suspected that it was the work of the same Harold Plumbwell. From the scrawled notes in the margins it was apparent that Aggie had studied it and verified some of the people and their dates, but not the crucial ones—the ones that mattered—the birth and ongoing life of Isabelle, and the immediate lineage of Plumbwell himself.

Tasha pulled a kitchen chair into the center of the living room and took up her cello. The instrument fit snuggly between her knees, dark and glowing, shapelier than the trees that made it. She bent over it with her bow. What should it be? Some music might serve as an angry, almost melodramatic, response to her confusion and fear—and when the drama ended, a fatigued relief. Then there was the kind of music that calmed her the way a pond in the woods might, but was too sweet to touch her fear, Schubert perhaps. She needed something tough and cleansing. Unfortunately, too many cello pieces were elegies, or might as well be, and she didn't think tears were the order of the day. So it was back to the Bach, which was wonderfully poised and clear sighted, but at the same time had something of dying and death in its bones, maybe because of the crucifixion that was so frequently its subject. It might make her feel whole again.

Coker's mother dropped Alex off at the museum that afternoon on the way to the barbershop with her son who very much needed a haircut. At the door to the Cyril Benning House, Alex heard Ms. Mulholland playing. He'd never been able to bring himself to interrupt her so he sat down on the stoop and waited. The music traveled across the grass and down the road, he could almost see it go. He wondered if Aggie heard it from her house and, if she did, why it hadn't helped her. He wondered why Ms. M was playing now and what was wrong. Something serious must have happened. When the music ended, he was puzzled to find the door to the house locked. It had never been before, not as far as he knew. He knocked and rang; he waited. He heard Winky trotting to the upstairs door, he heard Ms. Mulholland's step, strangely slowed, and the clop of her shoes as she came down the stairs to let him in. She almost never wore shoes inside; it was as if she'd kept them on so she could beat a speedy retreat if she had to. When she opened the door to him, she smiled her usual smile, but something wasn't right. He could see it in her eyes.

"Come on in, Alex. I made oatmeal cookies this morning. Would you like some milk?"

He took off his jacket and tossed it on the sofa, caught

Winky up onto his shoulder and sat down at the kitchen table. "What's happening, Ms. M?"

"Let me just get us settled. I need more coffee. You need milk. Then I'll tell you everything."

He noticed that she was drinking Jungle Madness again. Not a good sign.

She told him about the afternoon, except for her own comments about the murderer's future intentions and Sera's threat. They studied the contents of Aggie's envelope together.

"I'll bet Plumbwell found this genealogy online somewhere. I can't believe he made it himself. Are you going to confront Lori and Adrian about their con?"

She didn't answer him; instead she gazed down at her own shadowed reflection in her coffee. "Ms. M?" he asked. "Are you all right?"

"Not really." She looked up at him. "Alex, we need to talk about our partnership. I'm afraid it has to end."

"Did I do something wrong? I'll fix it. I didn't mean to."

"No, no. You've been a wonderful partner. We have to break it off because Mrs. Hamilton has put me directly in the way of danger."

"What does that have to do with anything? I can still help; nobody has to know."

"Sera may already know. When I eventually talk to Lori and Adrian, they may figure out that you've been working with me. I'm going to speak to my son about getting some protection, but

I don't think he can do much. You've got to stay away from me for a while, sweetie."

"It's just because I'm a kid, isn't it? Age discrimination is what it is. I'm just as good as a grown-up, except maybe for a grown-up guy with a gun."

"It's partly that you're a kid, yes. Your mother would die if she knew. But under the circumstances, I'd probably break off a partnership with anybody. Even a man with a gun. I can't risk your getting hurt, Alex."

"You wouldn't break it off with a man. Don't make things up. It's because I'm a kid. You know I've come up with stuff too. You'll miss me. I bet you won't even be able to solve it without me."

"That may be, Alex. But I have to try. Most of all I have to try to do what Aggie was doing and what she wanted me to continue doing, and find out who should inherit her estate. You know what happened to her. It could happen to me. It could happen to you too if you're still involved. I can't have that."

"Shit!" said Alex, and got up from the table.

"Alex! You know better than that."

"I hate this. I hope you can't find out anything without me. I bet you can't. You're just an old lady who doesn't even know how to use a computer. I'll solve the murder on my own. I don't need you, you'll see." Alex grabbed his jacket, slammed out of the room and bolted down the stairs, making every bit of noise he could.

That evening Stuart Mulholland sat in the same chair as Alex had in the afternoon, munching on some of the same batch of oatmeal cookies. He was beginning to get a pot, Tasha Mulholland noticed, and wondered if she should say anything. His face seemed to grow rounder every year. It had always been a baby face—soft, he'd never had much of a beard—with a subtle and permanent blush on the cheeks. His eyes were green like his father's, and for years she'd been careful not to look into them too deeply. He'd make the perfect Santa Claus: he had the twinkling smile and the loud ho ho. All he needed were the beard and the girth—and the girth was imminent. Even though he wore a silver badge, he didn't look like a lawman, not even in a town like Shrubsbury.

She'd told him everything Rupert Young, Esq. had said, including the remark about his providing protection for his mother. She didn't say anything about Alex or their investigations together; it was best that no one know about his involvement. It shouldn't be difficult to deflect any suspicions Lori or Adrian might entertain. They'd be busy trying to prove that Lori had a legitimate claim to Aggie's fortune. It didn't surprise her that Stuart didn't seem to know what to do about her predicament. He'd always been bewildered by her. He'd tried to stop her from jumping out of a plane when she was in her forties, from hiking the Long Trail when she was in her fifties, and from purchasing and riding one of those orphaned wild horses from the West when she was sixty. He'd never had any luck talking her out of anything she wanted to do and she was determined to fulfill Aggie's assignment to her. As nasty and unattractive as the woman was, it seemed to Tasha Mulholland that Aggie deserved better than she got at the end, and she, Tasha, was the only person who could make it right.

"Well, Mom, you've really got yourself into a spot this time," Stuart frowned into his cocoa.

"I didn't ask for this, Stuart. I was civil to the woman, that's all."

"Yeah. Sure. And I know better than to dissuade you from going along with a dead crazy lady. Let's see if we can set some ground rules."

"Oh, dear. What did you have in mind? Should I carry a gun?"

The idea of his mother with a gun made him cringe. "No. Knowing you, you'd use it when you shouldn't, and not when you should. But here's something simple: lock your doors. Whether you're here or not, and especially when you are, lock them."

"I can do that."

"I'd like to suggest that you include me or one of my deputies in any interviews you conduct."

"Don't be silly, Stuart. People won't talk if there's a policeman looking over my shoulder at them."

"Well then, telephone me every time you go to an interview and every time you finish one. And make certain that your subject knows you're doing it."

"That's possible," she said, but not with much enthusiasm. "But you know I work here and I talk to Lori and Adrian all the time."

"Okay. Try this. Check in with me every morning by phone. I'll come by every evening, or more often than that if you need me, and debrief you."

"That's good. I think that makes sense. And I'll see you a lot more than I have of late, won't I? Will your wife be upset by that? She can join you. She hasn't been here in a long time and I did make that cobbler she liked so well. I'm not sure why she hasn't come back. If it was the cello—I won't play it again. I promise."

"It doesn't matter, Mom. It's my job. I'll see you and it'll be good." He grinned broadly.

"Would you like some more cocoa, Stuart?" He nodded. He hadn't changed much in some ways, she thought. He was still a boy.

"If you feel threatened, even if you're worried that it's your imagination, I want you to call me."

"You're probably right, Stuart. I should. I'll try."

"Okay. One more rule I can think of. Never be alone with any of the people who could have murdered Mrs. Hamilton. Never. Always meet with them in public places: restaurants, soccer games, the museum only when it's open, whatever. What do you think?"

"I'll do my best."

"I hope so." He stirred his cocoa to cool it, and looked at his mother gravely. "I don't want anything to happen to you."

"I know, darling."

"One other thing we'll do to make sure you're safe. We'll change the lock on your door downstairs. I'll see that gets done tomorrow. I'll do it myself so no one will think anything's happening but a visit from your sheriff son."

"Thank you, Stuart."

"Does Alex need any protecting?"

"Why do you ask?"

"You and he have been such constant companions, and I know you've talked about the murder together. Maybe more than that. I remember when I was a kid. You always forgot that I was."

"Could you check on Alex? You're right. He thinks he's going to solve the murder. I am worried about him."

"I'll check to make sure he gets home after school and I'll have someone drive by every evening. I'm not sure what else we can do. Since he's a little kid, he'll probably be okay. No one will think of him as a threat. Don't scare him, but tell him to lock the doors and try not to be alone. Okay?"

"He's not speaking to me just now."

"Just as long as he's listening to you."

"Hmmmmm."

"So what are you doing tomorrow, Mom?"

"I might spend some time with Lori and Adrian. I don't want them to know that I'm the executrix yet, so I'm not sure. Mostly, I'll be doing research, probably in county records and the library downstairs. The weather's supposed to be nice; there should be visitors. I'll hold all my conversations in public places. Okay?"

"Okay. I'll call you in the morning, and I'll be here a little later to change the lock."

"Thank you, Stuart."

"You're welcome. Please do as I've suggested. Please don't take any chances. Remember what happened to Mrs. Hamilton. This killer's a vicious son of a gun. He means serious business."

XVII

Alex takes over

Riding the school bus home, trying to "yeah man" and "yo" Coker about Saturday's soccer game, Alex couldn't think of anything but his scheme for the afternoon. While his late and unlamented partner, Ms. Mulholland, fooled around with the false heirs to Aggie's fortune (a blind alley for sure), he planned to break the investigation wide open by bicycling to Major and Mrs. Shelton's house to check out the painting. He was pretty sure that Nathan Howe's art was more important to the case than they'd thought, and that the painting contained a secret. He wanted to look at it the same way he did Howe's portrait of Juliette, squinting and from different angles.

The eBay auction hadn't ended yet; in fact, it had a few days to go. There were three bidders, and the high bid had risen to three thousand dollars. It would probably go higher. Someone—maybe three someones—knew that the painting held a clue. Maybe about buried treasure—that seemed most likely. Maybe just proof of

Isabelle's birth—that didn't seem nearly as exciting. He wondered if the Major knew the painting was important. Ms. Mulholland might have some thoughts about that, but it didn't matter since she'd ended their partnership. She'd be sorry when he showed her how detective work should be done—not by raking grass with a nerd like Adrian or filing for a freaky lady.

As he got off the bus, he saw the deputy drive by. Clearly, the old lady had set the cops on him, but it shouldn't be hard to shake them. He made a show of being home, opening curtains, taking the garbage out. The cops drove by a second time, and then they seemed to be gone. He crept out the back door, looking up and down the road first, then grabbed his bike and headed out. He figured he had two hours of daylight and another half hour after that before his mother came home.

The roads were lined with deep ruts—it wasn't mud season, but it often seemed like it in Shrubsbury, and Alex wasn't certain where the Sheltons lived, just the road name from the phone book, but he knew where people with as much money as they probably had would be likely to hang a shingle, so it wasn't too long before he found the road. But even though the houses were big and classy, it was a lousy ride. High tips for the road men should have made it better. When the sun was on it, it was okay, but when the woods shaded it, the mud was worse because it hadn't dried and the shadows were long and cold and seemed to reach out to catch him. When it started going up in looping curves, it was harder to pedal. There were only a few houses on the way to the top, all of them with windows glinting and smoke coiling up from their pointy roofs. They were bigger than Coker's house and he knew there must be deer all over the hill, maybe even a bear or two, who knew? If his mother only had money. The Major was a jerk, and he had. Life wasn't fair.

At the very top of the hill, at the end of the road, was the Shelton house, the biggest of all and round with turrets. It was surrounded by fir trees, which made it easy for him to hide his bike and sneak up on the other side where the windows looked out on a vista of smoky hills smudged with early turning maples and pastures and lined with fences and dirt roads. The curtains were open and he could see Mrs. Shelton sitting in a red velvet chair, sipping on something that might have been alcoholic. Maybe that was what was wrong with her. He dodged around to the front of the house again and found a lawn chair to stand on so he could look through a garage window for the Major's car. No car. The man wasn't at home.

Alex dragged his bike out from the trees and took it to the front door with him, leaving it sprawled out—like he had just absolutely had it, and let go—a few feet from the front porch. Mrs. Shelton took her time coming to the door after he rang, but eventually she opened it. She was startled to see him. She'd only met him the one time on the day of Aggie's murder: he probably reminded her of how horrible it was to find a gory Aggie.

"Why, hello. Alex, isn't it? What are you doing here, Sweetie?"

"Hello, Mrs. Shelton. I went out riding after school and

ended up here. I'm so tired. I way overestimated how far I could go. I didn't know the hill would be so steep. Do you think you could give me a glass of water before I start back?"

"Of course. Why, you poor boy. You live way down near the Old Shrubsbury School House Museum, don't you? Why ever would you come this far?"

"I'm training for soccer and I need to build myself up. I have to work hard because if I don't get strong I'll end up being a nerd instead of a brain."

"I see," she said. "So you're already a brain but you want to be an athletic sort of brain and not a nerdy brain. Do I understand you?"

"You got it!" He was surprised. Without her husband, he liked her. She was even kind of pretty. He followed her to a kitchen bigger than the one in the high school and she ran some water from a special silver tap that was just for ice water. "Your house is amazing. It's round, isn't it? And it's got turrets. It's like a castle."

"Yes. We like it. Would you like me to show you around?"

"That would be great," he said, gulping down the water.

He followed her from room to room, each one with a curved wall and humongous windows. She chattered happily about the design of the house and how she'd suggested this rather than that, and how the house was a very happy place to be because of it. She was splendid, he thought— her eyes sparkling, her lips parted and moist, her breasts moving when she breathed. When they went into one of the turrets, she brushed against him. Her skin was cool and when she smiled and excused herself, he felt shaky all over and wondered if he was falling in love. He couldn't be sure, but maybe this was what it was like. Sure, she was older than he was, but her husband was even more years older than she was.

"I accidentally found you on eBay," he told her. "I know you love antiques." Even though he didn't know much about furniture, he could tell that nearly everything in the house was expensive and old.

"Yes, indeed. Why were you on eBay?"

"I was looking for things about Nathan Howe. I like his paintings in the museum. The portraits upstairs mostly. And that little painting of food on the third floor in the Shrubsbury Room. I want to be an artist when I grow up," he explained. It was one of those innocent lies even Ms. Mulholland might tell.

"Did you know I've written books about Nathan Howe?"

"No, ma'am. Are they too hard for someone twelve to read?"

"I don't know, probably not for a brain. I'll give you copies."

"Oh, hey. That's really nice of you. Do you talk about the landscape that's on eBay?"

"I do. In fact, the painting's downstairs. Would you like to see it?"

"Oh, yes. Very much."

Down the stairs again, round and round, she took him, to a basement room with lots of flowery still lifes, melodeons, and chairs. "These are our eBay items," she said. "And here's the Howe painting."

"Oh, wow." He moved back from it to stare at it. He really did like it, even more than he did on the computer screen. "It's awesome looking at it in reality."

She laughed. "Look as long as you like, Alex." He looked at it from one angle, and then another, and still another. She was very patient. Almost five minutes had passed when the Major appeared at the door.

"I see we have a visitor," he boomed.

"Yes, dear. Alex was riding his bike and ended up exhausted at our house. So now he's had a drink of water and we're looking at the house. He likes Nathan Howe paintings."

"Is that so? Most kids your age wouldn't give a damn for a painting by an old-fashioned twit. When I was your age I liked comic book art. What's with you, Alex?"

"He's a brain, dear."

"I see." He looked at Alex like he didn't believe a word of it. Not the Nathan Howe part. Not the brain part.

"I like comic books too, sir. Batman, and especially the Hulk." Alex was pretty sure from his face that the Major didn't know about the Hulk. "And the drawings in Rune Scape."

"What's that?"

"A computer game."

"Well, you're quite a kid, Alex. Would you like a ride home? It's getting late. Won't your mother be worried?"

"Yes, sir. She might be, but she's not home from work yet."

"It's getting dark. Let me drive you."

Alex tried to say no. He didn't like the Major, and he could tell the man didn't like him. His wife shouldn't have married him. At least his mother never married anyone mean. He and Mrs. Shelton followed Major Shelton back up the stairs and to the front door, Abigail Shelton smiling at him like she was apologizing for everything, while her husband put his bike in the trunk of his big purple-as-an-eggplant car. Alex slid into the front seat and waved goodbye.

"Come again, Alex. I enjoyed talking with you," Mrs. Shelton said in a sweet trilly voice.

"You like this car?" asked the Major as he drove down the mountain like it was a race track, even though the car was the size of a Mack truck. Ms. Mulholland had nothing on him.

"Very much, sir. I've never seen anything like it."

"That's the GPS you're looking at. You kids learn about that stuff in school now, I guess."

"Yessir."

"It's got a TV in back. And a bar. Even a coffee machine. Pretty snazzy, huh?"

"Yessir." Alex pressed himself into the seat as far back as he could, and planned how he might hurl himself out if the Major threatened him, but he heard the car doors lock themselves part way down the hill and knew he'd already blown it.

"I want you to know, Alex. I don't believe a word you say about how you turned up at our house. I know you're just a kid, but you're a smart kid. I hope you're smart enough to know that you and your old lady friend, Mulholland, had better stay out of my way. I've got a business to run, and I won't put up with any interference. You got that?"

"Yessir. But I'm not lying. I just turned up at your house without knowing what I was doing."

"Yeah, and found the Howe painting for the same reason. Just be careful. You're not that good a liar, kid."

XVIII

Nathan Howe's house

School went on forever the next day. It was a worse drag because Alex had plans. According to Mrs. Shelton's book, Nathan Howe painted the landscape about the same time as he painted Juliette and her doctor husband. In 1838. The painting-over wasn't as clear as in Juliette's portrait, but when he squinted at Howe's painting from the right angle a flock of sheep under a tree and next to the road turned into a house. When he looked closely, he could see that Howe had painted the house out with the sheep, and the house, like the baby, was coming back. Even though the road didn't go up the hill any more and it had been, he guessed, about one hundred and sixty-five years since the painting was made, he wanted to find Nathan Howe's house.

He told his mother he was going to the museum to hang out with Ms. Mulholland after school, and she said fine, she'd pick him up. He got off the school bus at his usual stop near the museum then moved as fast as he could because he didn't want his old lady ex-partner to spot him. Chances were, she'd set the cops on him again. Once he got across from Aggie's house, and to where the trees were, he was okay. He knew the old road went straight up the side of the hill. The house, Nathan's house disguised as sheep, was about halfway up, so if he walked in a straight line from Aggie's house, he should find it. He had a compass to keep him from wandering off course.

Ms. Mulholland would have known how long it had been since the road was used. He guessed it was probably a hundred years ago. There was no sign of it now, of course; trees and bushes had grown up everywhere. But the flock of sheep that covered Howe's house had been next to a very big tree. It might have been a beech or an oak, or maybe just a large maple. Since that was one hundred and sixty-five years ago, the tree might be gone. Or it could have grown and become massive. There were trees like that around. It might have, by now, become a huge hollow stump. Whatever it was now, he wanted to find it and a cellar hole next to it with some tired apple trees and maybe a lilac. He wasn't sure what a lilac looked like when it wasn't flowering, but most old cellar holes seemed to have both apples and lilacs, which was pretty cool when he thought about it.

It was hard to see where halfway up the hill was when he was in a bunch of trees, but when he got to the top of the hill, he knew he'd missed it, so he started back down, feeling a little bummed. There was nothing but scrub and trees everywhere. No big tree, dead or alive, no cellar hole, no apple trees. He was almost ready to give up, when he heard voices.

"So you're going to build a house on this acreage?"

"Yes. Right on Nathan's old cellar hole, I hope."

How did his old lady ex-partner find this place? What was she doing with Nick?

Hiding in a stony depression in the ground behind a bush, Alex waited for Ms. Mulholland and Nick as they came closer and closer until it occurred to him like a bolt that he was probably hiding in Nathan Howe's cellar hole and that they were going to find him there. He climbed out fast, rocks falling and sliding—they had to hear him crashing through the tangle—and found another hiding place, this time on the other side of Nathan's lilac bush.

"What in the devil was that?" asked Nick.

"Probably a deer but it was small. Maybe a fox. I just caught a glimpse of it," said Ms. Mulholland, and he knew she'd seen him.

"So this is it, Ms. Mulholland," said Nick Crafts. "It wasn't such a hard climb, was it? This is where Nate Howe lived."

"Of course, he lived on what was like a highway then. If you build here, you'll live in the woods with the nearest road three-quarters of a mile down the hill. You'll have to build a long driveway before you're ready to build a house. You're going to need money, and lots of it."

"That's okay. I'll find it. And it will still be easier for me than it was for the folks back then."

"Maybe not. They didn't have a woods to contend with; they'd already cut down most of the forest. What about water? Is there a well?"

"I haven't found it yet, but I'm sure he must have had one."

"And electricity?"

"A bridge I'll cross when I come to it. I might just buy a generator."

"You'll be ready to volunteer at all the museum functions?"

"Positively," he grinned at her with his charming grin.

Ms. Mulholland laughed the funny throaty laugh Alex used to like when he liked her. "So Nick, tell me. How did you find out that Howe had a house up here?"

"I discovered the cellar hole when I was a kid, and I always thought it was where I would like to build someday. It was hard to find land records going back that far. In fact, on the old maps the property belongs to the Whittingtons. The painting of the road that Major Shelton has for sale suggests that the land belonged to Howe since Howe painted it and apparently built the house. Then this past summer Agatha Hamilton confirmed that the cellar hole had been Howe's and that the property was now hers. She agreed to sell the land to me if we did an archaeological dig on it."

"Why did she want a dig?"

"I don't know. Just because it's the site of one of the first houses, I guess."

"I'm sure you're right. She did love history. How did you find out about the painting? Did Aggie tell you about it?"

"Yeah. I'm trying to buy it on eBay, but I'm being outbid by a couple of people. I'd love to put it in my living room after I build the house."

"Did you know Aggie when your father and mother lived here?"

"Yes, but as a little boy knows an adult. And, since she was a scary adult, even less than that."

"Were you aware that your father had an affair with Aggie?"

"Oh, yes."

"You remember it?"

"I remember all the fights about it. It's why we moved."

"Did he get her pregnant?"

"Oh my God, I hope not. Did he?"

"Just my nosiness. I have no idea."

"So I might have a half sister or brother?"

"Maybe. It's just vague speculation."

They began to walk back towards the road. "If I do, do you have any ideas who he or she might be, and where?"

"I don't. Not a one, Nick." She said something else, but Alex couldn't hear it. He was glad they were leaving. His nose was itching and he wanted to sneeze. Besides, he was mad enough to spit. How had Ms. Mulholland found out about Nick and gotten him to show her the cellar hole? Did she believe him, that he just happened to want to buy the place where Howe lived? Was there a treasure here? Why else would Old Aggie have wanted an archaeological dig? He didn't believe she loved history that much. Why did Nathan Howe make his mystery paintings? What was he hiding? Was it a treasure? It had to be a treasure; treasures were what people hid. What else could it be?

He'd looked at Mrs. Shelton's books the night before, but there wasn't much about Nathan's life, just his painting. Not even whether he had a family, although there was a reference to an illegitimate child in Vermont. There was also a self-portrait. Alex studied it a long time, trying to see his own face in Howe's. Neither he nor Nathan were handsome like Dr. Whittington, or at least Howe didn't paint himself that way so he probably wouldn't have painted Alex that way. Ms. M had explained subjectivity to him. Dr. Whittington might not have been handsome either; maybe Nathan Howe just thought he was, or painted him that way so he would feel good about himself and pay more for the painting. Maybe Juliette wasn't beautiful to anyone but Howe.

Not likely.

He thought he looked something like Nathan Howe or, as he'd started to call him, Nate, or my man Nate. The full cheeks, the light brown eyes, the dimple in the chin, the high forehead. Maybe Ms. Mulholland guessed right when she said Alex should find out about his genealogy. Nathan Howe just might be his great-great-great-or-even-one-or-two-more-greats-granddad. Here he was sitting in the man's basement looking at the tumbled stones, wondering what the house looked like. They'd had archaeologists at camp last summer. Alex tried to look at the cellar hole the way an archaeologist would. It was small for sure. A rough little house with a kitchen, a living room and a tiny bedroom with a rope bed like the ones in the museum. Maybe a desk. Nate might have got the desk from Evensong who probably felt sorry for him because he couldn't make any money painting and his house was so rickety. There must have been an outhouse somewhere in the back, and a vegetable garden. Without quite knowing why, Alex knew Nate sat every evening on the porch and looked down the road and across the pasture and the fields, aware that Juliette and the baby were there in that second story window, looking back at him. The woman he loved and her baby. Alex didn't know much about sex and that kind of love, less even than his mother thought he did, but he knew how it felt to care about someone and want to touch her—just the day before he'd felt that way about Mrs. Shelton—and he knew that was what might have been going on here.

Whether Alex was related to his man Nate or not, he felt like he was. He imagined the tipped back chair Nate sat on, the pipe he was smoking, one made of polished piano wood like his father used to smoke. He listened to an owl hoot far back in the woods, a dog bark at the Clemson farm a mile away, a chickadee in the tree above him; nothing was much different from when Nate was here, just more trees and less house. No road. He started walking back; his mother would be picking him up soon. He didn't want to see Ms. Mulholland so he'd have to make a run for it when he got out of the woods. Maybe go over to the church and hide.

But Ms. M was there, sitting on a rock at the side of the road, waiting for him. "Hi, Alex. I know you're not talking to me, but I thought you should know I'm pretty impressed that you found Nathan Howe's house."

He stopped and looked at her with the darkest scowl he

could muster. He wouldn't talk. It didn't matter what she said.

"You must have looked at Howe's painting. Slipped past your police guard yesterday and went to the Sheltons, I'll bet. I'm really curious, Alex. Is it like Juliette's painting? Did you squint at it?"

"The sheep are fading and the house is showing," he answered her, disappointed in himself for telling, but too proud to have discovered it not to say.

"I'll be darned. Really extraordinary, isn't it? And if they were painted about the same time, the paint might begin to fade in the same month of the same year. Especially since the museum records I looked at today show that both paintings were on the fourth floor for most of the time since they were painted. Just fading away together for years and years. "

"You mean the landscape belongs to the museum? Maybe Major Shelton stole it? Maybe that's why he threatened me."

"Oh, Alex. What am I going to do with you?"

"Take me back as a partner?"

"I guess I'd better, so I can keep track of you. But we have to be very careful. No one must know we're working together. Not even Stuart. God, he'd dress me down if he knew." She was so consternated (one of his summer words), he liked her all over again. "Either the Sheltons stole it, or they're dealing in stolen property. Try to stay away from them; they could be dangerous."

"Not her. Just him. She's different."

"Hmmmmm. Maybe. Tell me what you think about Nick. Is he telling the truth?"

"I don't know. I want him to be."

"What do you think Nathan Howe was doing in these two paintings, painting out a baby and his own house?"

"He must have been trying to erase his existence in Juliette's life. That's sort of like making up stories, isn't it? But Mrs. Shelton's second book says he had an illegitimate daughter, and that must be the baby in the painting."

"Mrs. Shelton's second book?"

"Yeah. *Vermont and Vermont Painters*. See, you should have stayed my partner and you'd know all about it."

"It never occurred to me to look for another book by the woman. Oh, Alex. You're right. I should have stayed your partner."

"And besides, I think I'm related to him. I'm a Howe too, my mother says. Up there on the hill I felt like I knew him, like he was my granddad many times removed." He watched a question taking form on her face. "You think I'm bonkers."

"No, I think everything you say makes sense. Do you have a soccer game tomorrow?"

"Yeah. In the morning."

"Maybe we could persuade your mom to take us to your Grandmother Howe's in the afternoon."

XIX

The visit to Grandma Howe

Alex couldn't figure out how Ms. M did it, but she'd talked his mother into it. Ms. Mulholland had always been good at selling stuff, especially to his mother who was a softie around old and venerable ladies. So after Coker and he together lost the soccer game by flipping the ball off the field into some tall grass so everyone had to look forever to find it again, Donna Churchill, Ms. Mulholland and Alex headed for North Troy to visit Alex's paternal grandmother who he barely remembered but who his mother always said was really mean and knew a lot about his dad's genealogy.

While his mother drove, she and Ms. M chattered about making a quilt show for the museum, so the trip wasn't exactly exciting. No speeding around hairpin curves, not even any talk about his father and his father's mother, which is what he would have liked. His father had left when Alex was just a baby. He didn't want women in his life any more, not his wife, not his mother. Alex didn't know why his dad also left him, but he guessed he was too little to have made much of an impression. His mother almost never wanted to talk about his father, which is one reason he supposed he never saw Grandma Howe. And the reason he was surprised she was up for the trip.

"You'll be all right seeing Mrs. Howe again?" Ms. Mulholland finally asked her.

"I've matured since the last time I saw her. She can't get to me anymore. And Alex should have the opportunity to at least know about his father," said Donna Churchill. Then she went back to talking about quilts.

Alex tried to concentrate on his and Ms. Mulholland's case, but he couldn't. So he watched the hills flatten into long sloping fields, and counted Jersey cows and Holsteins to see which outnumbered which. Heading toward Jay Peak, watching it grow higher and higher, the country felt like the Old West. No snow on the mountain, of course. Not yet. Alex's class was going skiing at Jay in December, and Coker and he were going to try free styling there for the first time.

The highway dipped down and Alex began to get uncomfortable. "Couldn't we stop and get milk shakes or something?" he asked as they approached the snack shack on the side of the road.

"You just had lunch at home," his mother responded. "Don't be nervous. It'll be okay."

"Yeah, after all the things you've said about her, I'm not

supposed to be nervous?"

"She's just different. And she may have changed, she may even be nice. Although I suppose that's not likely. But I haven't seen her for years."

They drove by Go Go Trucking, the town's biggest industry, its huge shiny trucks parked neatly in a yard by a warehouse, then past the turnoff to Canada. It was only a mile to the border. Alex wished fleetingly that the women would choose foreign travel over Grandma Howe's. He had a vague memory of Grandma Howe as an ancient woman, leaning over him, cackling, devouring him with her eyes. Like the witch in *Hansel and Gretel*.

North Troy was bigger than Shrubsbury, but not so that it mattered. A couple of restaurants and a grocery, an auto repair, a school, several streets of Victorian homes and miscellaneous hybrids of other styles. Grandma Howe lived in the least attractive house by far at the end of a dead-end road where yellow dirt dribbled into a sea of scrub. The house itself was a marvel of flaking paint and crumbling curlicues. To get to the front door they had to step across a fallen picket gate and hike down a broken-up walkway through a yard where statues of donkeys, pink flamingos and angels with their wings at full mast lurked in the tall browning weeds. To the side and in front of a crumbling wraparound porch two naked wooden boys were bent over with their rear ends in the air, apparently peeing into some dying asters. "So decorous," murmured Ms. Mulholland.

Immediately above the porch stairs, attached to the

gingerbread that once ran all the way around the house but now intermittently disappeared, was a wasp's nest, so they tiptoed up the stairs one by one. The only thing on the porch was a dried-up rocker, with a cushion almost faded white. Two striped cats lay in a heap on it. They stared at the visitors for a moment, but finding them uninteresting, yawned, stretched, and closed their eyes again. Alex's mother pressed the doorbell. Nothing happened. She knocked and a dog started barking and scratching at the other side of the door as if he were going to tear it down and tear them up, or maybe it was more than one dog because it seemed to Alex that the sound was as loud as a pack of them. The cats on the rocker came to attention and sat straight up, their fur turned stiff. Either they planned to join forces with the dogs or make a run for it when the door burst open. At Ms. Mulholland's suggestion, Alex and his mother prepared to hide their faces in their arms in case the dogs stirred up the wasps.

Behind the door, there were muffled commands and the sound of what could be someone wrestling the animals to the floor and dragging them away. At last it was quiet, just neighborhood birds twittering, a car rumbling by, nothing at all. "I wonder if I should knock again," Alex's mother said apprehensively.

"Aye?" growled a voice so old it might have been prehistoric, and the door opened just enough for a skinny woman, ancient as the fairy tale witch, to peer out. "Is that you, Donna Churchill Howe?" Most of Grandma Howe's face was lost in a squeeze box of wrinkles and whiskers, like the ancient table melodeon at the museum, except for her big-as-saucers watery blue eyes. She stood there, with her chin jutting out, sizing them up one by one, then wiping her hands on her stained apron, as if she were a fighter getting ready to take them on.

"Well, come on in. Now that you've come all this way you might just as well." She opened the door wider but not wide enough and they had to flatten themselves against the jamb to get by her. She slammed the door behind them so that the glass in all the windows in the house rattled, and they were left in the dark hallway, glad to be away from the wasps, not knowing whether to keep going but not really wanting to because the house stunk of kitty litter—as Ms. Mulholland would have said if it were polite to do so—to high heaven. They could hear cats running and tumbling somewhere in front of them. "Well, keep going, all of you, there's nothing going to bite you," said Grandma Howe. So they did.

At the end of the hallway they came out into a living room with big stuffed chairs decorated with yellowing antimacassars, and little tables covered with china cups, porcelain figurines and old photographs. There was an ugly brown piano on one wall, and Alex wondered if his father played it when he was growing up. He looked for pictures of him but he didn't want to upset his mother, so he was circumspect and careful and didn't really search. There were cats everywhere, and they all seemed happy. They nestled in the gray shag rug and lay on their backs on a purple love seat, toasting themselves in the powdered sunlight that poured through the window. Two black cats with glowing golden eyes were perched on the top of a bookshelf, next to a painting that seemed familiar. Another Howe?

While his mother and Ms. Mulholland sat down carefully, trying not to crush a cat or raise dust, Alex walked over and looked at the painting. Nathan Howe's signature was in the corner. It was probably of Nate Howe's wife and child. Alex wanted to squint at it, but he no longer thought it likely all of Nathan Howe's paintings had paintings-out on them.

"You like that painting, Alex Jr.? It was done by your many-greats-grandfather."

So he was a descendent of Nate Howe. "Did my dad grow up here?" he asked. This might be his only chance to find out something about his father since his mother wouldn't talk and the old lady didn't look long for this world.

"Yes, he did that."

"Mother Howe," his mother said, "We wanted to find out something about Alex's genealogy on his father's side."

"Yup," is all she said. He could see that she didn't like his mother even a little bit. She turned and eyed Ms. Mulholland like she might be from another planet. "And you brought re-enforcements, Donna Churchill. Who's this?" she snapped, glaring at Ms. M with her huge wet eyes.

"I'm Tasha Mulholland, Mrs. Howe. I'm a friend of Donna's and Alex's."

"Hmmmph. I hate to think the stories she's told you about my boy." The old woman stood up. She must have been taller once.

Now she was shorter than Alex. "Would you folks like some tea or something? I ordered in a root beer for the boy here. His dad always liked root beer."

His mother and Ms. M made sounds that might mean yes, and she started to walk towards where he guessed the kitchen must be. Then she stopped abruptly. "Mulholland. Did you have a relative owned a livery over to Jay?"

Ms. Mulholland smiled her most pleasant smile. Alex saw her cross her fingers for good luck, hoping her ex-husband's dad wasn't someone the old lady hated. "Yes, I did."

"Good man, he was. Good man," she said, as if she was glad for a respectable guest, although she wouldn't have expected it. She started to move toward the kitchen again. "You. Alex Jr. Come help me with the tea things." He jumped.

The kitchen was at least as old as she was. It had a big black wood stove, and the sink had a pump handle. Empty cat food cans were stacked on one side of the counter, all washed like they might come in handy for something he couldn't think what. "You remember your dad, Alex?" she asked.

"Sort of."

"There's none of us knows where he's at now. He might be dead, far as we know."

"Why did he leave?"

"He was unhappy with your mother, is what it was."

"I guess he didn't like me much either."

"I don't think it was that. Anyway, it was passed down to him that he'd leave. All the Howe men are like that. His father did it and his father before him. Someday you'll do the same."

Not if he had a kid, Alex thought. But he didn't say it because he knew they needed to placate Grandma Howe (one of Ms. Mulholland's summer words).

She poured out his root beer and put the glass on an old Coca-Cola tray with a sugar bowl and cream pitcher. "You take that in. I've got the teacups and the pot." The tea was already made and ready in a big pot with pink flowers all over it. The cups were chipped but they matched. Poor thing, he thought. She's trying to impress my mom. No way it's going to work.

The grown-ups were settled with their tea and Alex was sipping his root beer before old Mrs. Howe said more. "Okay, then. What do you want to know about Alex Jr.'s ancestors?"

"We want to know if the painter of that painting, Nathan Howe, is Alex's however-many-greats ancestor, and whether you have the line recorded so that he can have a copy of it."

"Well, yes I do believe he is and yes, Alex may have my chart of it. I researched it out with his dad's grandpa a long time ago, and he'd done the same with his grandpa."

"What was the name of Nathan Howe's daughter?" asked Ms. Mulholland, deciding not to wait to ask questions since Grandma Howe was volatile and they might not be welcome for long. She looked up at the young girl in the painting who resembled her mother too much to be Juliette's daughter, with long chestnut hair and a strange half smile that seemed made up.

"Charlotte," said Grandmother Howe.

"Not Isabelle."

"Never Isabelle."

"Was there an Isabelle? Did he also have a daughter, Isabelle?"

"Yes. You think I never heard that story, aye? I've heard it and presuming on the nature of the male sex, I'm sure it's gospel, but Isabelle would be illegitimate, wouldn't she, and she wouldn't have anything to do with Alex here."

"Do you know anything about Isabelle's mother, Juliette?"

"I know that the painter Howe fooled around just like my husband did, and like Donna Churchill's. Only Donna was too righteous to leave it be. She had to make trouble."

"What happened to Isabelle?" Ms. Mulholland asked quickly so that the old lady wouldn't have time to rile up Alex's mother.

"I haven't any idea. Maybe her ma tried to raise her; maybe she pitched her. Howe didn't keep her."

"Did you ever hear that she died in infancy?"

"Some say she did; some not. Her ma died when Isabelle would have been just a tyke, I think." She sat there thinking, sipping her tea, like there was something else to say. A fat gray cat jumped onto Alex's lap, stretched out, purred and kneaded his legs.

"I remember there was a story... Her eyes were fixed on something past, almost as if they'd turned inside out and were looking into some interior place where the past was stored like a movie and she was watching the rerun. "Maybe she didn't die because I heard a tale once where she was growed and came back

148

to see her aunt and her aunt wouldn't give her the time of day."

"Audrey. Juliette's sister."

"Might be. I don't remember the name. 'Course both Juliette and her cuckolded husband were long dead by then." Alex wanted to ask what cuckolded meant, but he thought he'd better not since Ms. Mulholland had got the old lady talking and she might quit if she got interrupted.

"You have a remarkable memory for detail, Mrs. Howe. Do you remember who told you that tale?"

"Had to be my old man's granddad. Nowhere else I could have got it."

"So Nathan Howe lived out his life in New Hampshire," Alex's mother said so sweetly he couldn't believe it. "When did the Howes come back to Vermont?"

"Not 'til my grandpa's generation. Not that you really care, Donna Churchill. Out of sight, out of mind where my son was concerned, eh?"

"You don't remember any other stories about Juliette or Isabelle?" Ms. Mulholland interrupted again.

"No. They were never exactly my concern." She had decided she'd told them enough, Alex guessed, because she turned to him and asked if he'd like to see some pictures of his dad. Alex said yes. He was sure his mother wasn't too happy about it, but tough, a guy should know something about his father no matter how bad a guy he was and how his mom felt. Grandmother Howe brought over a big book where all the pictures were glued onto stiff black pages with little black corner pockets. Mostly the pictures were in color, only the color was draining out of them and Alex's father, who looked like him, was disappearing like Howe's sheep in his painting, only nothing else, no one else, was underneath. He was a baby on Grandma Howe's lap when she was pretty, with Grandpa Howe standing behind her looking proud. It was hard to get used to old people being young—like Aggie who used to be movie star glamorous, and now the old Mrs. Howe who in the album looked like maybe she'd been a high school cheerleader and his granddad a football player.

"Did my dad play sports?" Alex asked, hoping that he'd inherited genes that would make him a good soccer player.

"Nah. He had flat feet and couldn't run worth a damn."

Alex was alarmed. Did he have flat feet? He didn't know feet could be flat. It was scary how much he looked like his father, he thought, staring at the young man in the pictures.

"He was a charmer, your dad was. Just like your granddad. Not an honest bone in his body, but a charmer."

"Why didn't you grow him up to be honest?" Alex asked, suddenly tired of the insults against his father, first from his mother, and now from his grandmother.

"It's all in the genes, Alex Jr. I tried. Didn't do no good."

"Did Granddad leave my father?"

"Yeah, he did that."

"How old was my pop when his dad left?"

"Oh, he was near grown. Wasn't no man gonna leave me with

the sole raising of a child. I wasn't like poor Donna Churchill. Not a bit."

What clinched it for Alex was a picture of his father fishing with his grandfather. You'd think Alex Sr. could have hung around long enough to take him fishing. He didn't want to be a Howe. He wished he could start over and choose his own father. He was glad his mother had made him into a Churchill. "Shouldn't we go now?" he asked, standing up so that the fat gray cat slid to the floor with a plop and a meow came out without his meaning to make it.

"We can do that if you want, Alex," said his mother.

"You're a bitch, Donna Churchill. Turned the boy against me, haven't you? I should have known better than to let you folks come. You go. You want to go, you go. Don't worry about me. Next time you come, I'll be dead."

"Do you have a copy of Alex's genealogy, Mother Howe? He really wants it."

"It's made," she sniffed. "I made it for him before you came. Here, Alex Jr." She shoved an envelope at him.

"Thank you," Alex said. He felt himself stiffening.

"Don't open it now. I want you out. Out, all of you. Now."

Alex followed his mother and Ms. Mulholland to the door and was about to leave the dark hallway with them for the bright white light outside, when the old lady put her skinny arms around him and crushed him to her, all her jutting-out bones poking him like too many elbows. "You're all that's left of my boy. You take care of yourself, Alex Jr.," she said in a gravelly voice, her breath smelly and hot on his neck.

Alex looked down at her upturned face with water running down the creased cheeks from her big pooling-up eyes, nodded, and got out of her hands as quickly as he could. He didn't look back but when he hopped over the gate, he heard her slam the door, so hard this time that glass broke—he didn't know where. He scrambled into the car and closed his eyes so he wouldn't have to look at the house again, and they drove down the dusty street where all the houses look blurred because he was tearing up like some kind of little kid.

XX

Nathan Howe's watercolor

After Alex finished his homework on Sunday, he bicycled over to the museum. Across the road from Ms. Mulholland's house, church services at Shrubsbury Church were just ending. He could hear the organist pumping hard on the old Estey organ while the congregation filed out, chattering and laughing to a thumping postlude. Church bells rang. He counted. Twelve rings. Ms. Mulholland was out on her knees in back of the Cyril Benning House, cleaning up the garden for the winter. She looked up and grinned at him from under the wide beribboned brim of a straw hat when he rolled up. They were good again. "Hi, Alex. How're things?"

"They're pretty okay, Ms. M. Do you need any help?"

"I'm just about finished cleaning out after the asters." She crackled the purple suns of flowers in her hands. "Then I need some coffee and cookies. How about you?"

"Are we going to sleuth some more today?"

"There's plenty to do. We need to know more about Isabelle Howe," she said, looking up at him. "Are we sure she was illegitimate? Can we be sure she survived her childhood? Your Grandmother Howe said the story of her return to Shrubsbury was just that—a story."

"Everyone was lying then just like they do now," Alex complained. "I don't think we're ever going to figure it out."

"It's not quite that bad. There are no birth records for Isabelle, no matter who her father was. But since there aren't, it's less likely that Dr. Whittington was her father than that Howe was. A legitimate birth would have been celebrated and recorded. An illegitimate birth might have been ignored and even hidden. We haven't looked in the town records yet to see if a baby's birth was recorded for any Howe relatives. If there was, if her name was Isabelle, maybe they took the baby."

"Because Nathan Howe wasn't married yet, was he?"

"Not according to anything I can find. Not according to Abigail Shelton. I think that if the baby was illegitimate, both Howe and the Whittingtons were intent on keeping it a secret. So I don't think we'll find a record of her birth. Howe's paintings may be as close as we're going to get to the story of what happened. He painted out the baby, he painted out his house. Any record of his dalliance with Juliette was obliterated. Their daughter's existence was covered up."

"It's a good story, isn't it, Ms. M? I hope it's true."

"Hmmmmmm. Very good story. Prize-winning historical

fiction. And I suppose there could be more paintings. The story could go on and on. Coffee table books full."

"Do you think the Sheltons have more?"

"I don't know. Perhaps, since they're apparently privy to this whole mystery and want to sell to the highest bidder. You were in their house. Did you see everything?"

"I'm not sure I did. There wasn't another Howe painting with the eBay stuff." He tried to think his way through the Shelton's house. Something about his walk-through was troubling him. Howe's watercolor! He remembered he told Mrs. Shelton....

"Oh, hey, Ms. Mulholland. What about the little watercolor in the Shrubsbury town room?"'

She sat there with broken vegetation limp in her hands, staring at him as if he'd just said something really far out. "Is there one?"

"Yes, ma'am."

"By Howe?"

"Yep. It's hard to read the signature. It's a watercolor and it isn't very impressive. It's faded and little and it's just a picture of food. You know, like a still life," he said, remembering the French paintings of fruits and flowers she'd shown him last summer.

"I never knew. You never cease to amaze me, Alexander Churchill. Let's go look at it." She got to her feet and headed off. "You say it's of food?"

She was walking so fast, he had trouble keeping up with her. "Yeah, it's just of food." Holy moly, he realized, almost running, maybe it was of a root cellar. "It must be of a root cellar. It's food."

Ms. M was mumbling to herself. "Why that room? I've always avoided that room because most of the stuff has no story. I don't even remember the painting. Some detective you are, Tasha Mulholland. If it weren't for this child, you wouldn't know anything." Alex grinned, running just at her heel.

"Who else knows it's there? Aggie must have known?" asked Tasha Mulholland.

"It's in a corner looking unimportant. Maybe Old Aggie knew, maybe Mr. Dabney, but no one else I'll bet." He didn't say anything to Ms. M about Mrs. Shelton. He didn't want to worry her yet. Maybe Mrs. Shelton didn't hear him. Or care if she did.

"Not 'Old Aggie.' Mrs. Hamilton, Alex. Remember? Adrian's in his office counting money. Lori's in the gift shop. Let's go quickly."

They made so much noise going up the stairs, they would have scared someone if there'd been anyone to scare. In the corner, where Alex remembered the painting, was a rectangular space on the wall where it had been and wasn't any more. All that remained was a yellowing label: "Root Cellar at the Shrubsbury School."

Ms. M plopped down on a child's chair where no one was supposed to sit, and Alex dropped to the dusty floor beside her, both of them staring at the wall, tears beginning to trail down their cheeks. Detectives weren't supposed to cry but sometimes, said Ms. M, you just feel so snookered, there's nothing else to do.

Sadly, Alex told Ms. Mulholland about Mrs. Shelton. They

agreed that the Sheltons probably took it yesterday while they were with Grandma Howe.

"I think," she said, "that we should keep quiet about the fact that it's missing. We can look at yesterday's guest book to see if the Sheltons were here. Don't worry, sweetie. Mrs. Shelton is a very nice woman and I would probably have told her about it too. If I'd known. Which I should have and you did. If they sell the watercolor to someone, if that person comes looking for something, then we have a chance of discovering a clue we wouldn't have if you had kept what you knew to yourself. I can't imagine the Sheltons will put it on eBay since that would be tantamount to advertising thievery, but check when you get home."

It was while they were sitting there in the half shadows of the Shrubsbury town room, mourning the loss of "Root Cellar at the Shrubsbury School," that they heard someone coming slowly up the stairs. Ms. Mulholland put a finger to her lips; Alex nodded. Nick Crafts and Lori Chickering were talking together in earnest tones. For a moment, Alex worried that he and Ms. M would be discovered, but the two kept talking and walking, up to the fourth floor, near to the sky, and near to the portrait of Juliette and her baby. Together, Ms. Mulholland and Alex crept out into the hallway and halfway up the stairs so they could hear what was being said.

"You see, Lori. There it is, the picture of the baby Isabelle."

"How in God's name did she get there when she's never been there before?"

"Nathan Howe painted her there and then he painted her out. She's re-emerging."

"And that re-emerging figure, that badly painted infant, is what Aggie was going to use to prove another line and you at the end of it?"

"Yes."

"How close did she get?"

"Close enough. I think the executrix will be pleased with the evidence when it's revealed to her. I've had to move slowly because the proofs of my ancestry are delicate. Besides, I don't want to appear greedy."

"Of course not, you wily man. Are you really certain that Ms. Mulholland will award you Aggie's house and fortune?"

"It does look like it. Just as Aggie hoped."

"Why couldn't she just leave you the money?"

"She wanted to believe we had a blood connection. That blood connection was important to her."

"I'm still jealous, you know. Of you and her. I know it sounds ridiculous, but I am."

"Oh, darling Lori. Don't be silly. She was a crazy old lady with delusions trying to relive the past."

"And you did your best to encourage her delusions."

"Of course. Why not? They made her happy. She wasn't long for this world anyway."

"You say that with so much certainty, Nicky. Her doctors could have been wrong. She might have just been trying to win your sympathy."

"I don't think so. She already had it."

"Who do you think killed her?"

"I don't know. Since it wasn't me and it wasn't you, I don't know. I am right that it's not you, aren't I? Perhaps it's Sera Hamilton. If they found her out, I'd be very happy. It would be good to be rid of that scary lady. But I'd be almost as happy if it were Adrian."

"I'd never have killed her. I wanted her for a mother, for God's sake."

"Give it up, Lori. You're talking to me. You and your mother fixation already."

No one said another word for a full minute. Alex wrinkled up his nose: they were probably kissing. How could his hero choose a girl who was so unfortunate looking is what Ms. Mulholland would say? And silly besides. But there was something else. He wasn't prepared to hear Nick sound hard. Maybe he was just playing along with Lori, hoping she'd slip up and own up to her guilt.

"Soon, you and I will be together with all the money we could ever want," murmured Nick. They were walking towards the door and the hiding detectives. Ms. Mulholland was down the stairs and pressed behind the door of the Coventry room faster than the blink of an eye. Mired in lost illusions, Alex was slower.

"Hey, Alex. What are you doing here?" asked Nick as Alex tried to find his way back into the Shrubsbury Room.

"I'm doing some dusting for Ms. M," he answered. "I didn't know you were up here; when I heard footsteps I thought it might be her. I'm supposed to be much further along than I am."

"She's not that much of a taskmaster, is she?"

"You'd be surprised."

"I would," Lori said. "You were spying, weren't you, Alex?"

"No, Miss Chickering. Why would I do that?"

Nick laughed. "Get out of here, bro. Be quick about it. Be careful and don't get caught next time. You never know what might happen if you do."

Alex decided it was the better part of valor to be scared and made a fast exit ahead of them, down the stairs and out the kitchen door, his words trailing behind him: "Hey, man, I didn't mean to spy. Honest, I didn't." Ms. M. hunkered down in the Coventry Room and waited. When Alex was gone Nick murmured, "That damn kid is as nosy as the old lady."

"I think they share nearly everything. If you got rid of one, you'd have to get rid of the other."

"Yeah, you're right," said Nick. "I'm just ranting." They continued on their way downstairs, and a few minutes later Ms. M heard the door open and close. She sat there in the dust of the little town room, noticing that this time she wasn't afraid at all. She was angry. One thing was certain. If she could do what she wanted—and she probably couldn't—she wouldn't award anything of Aggie's to Nick or Lori.

Nick climbed into his truck and sat quietly, watching Alex sitting on the steps of the Cyril Benning House. He liked kids.

He wished he'd been less stern. The kid was just a kid; he didn't pose any threat.

He wasn't as certain how he felt about Lori. She was always so needy. The mother thing was especially annoying. Aggie was the last person you'd expect someone like Lori to want for a mother. Sure, she'd always been nice to him. Gone out of her way for him because of his dad. Aggie was loyal to the memory of the only love she'd apparently ever experienced. Sad, that.

But Lori. She'd have stopped seeing him to try to keep Aggie's affection. She'd said at the time that it was because of him, to encourage his and Aggie's relationship so that he'd inherit. But that was incidental, he knew, and he didn't know what to make of it. There was something about Lori that he couldn't help loving—a manic helplessness that he related to. He couldn't decide whether her problems—again, the mother thing—canceled out what he cared about in her. He'd hoped that Aggie's death would help them both. The inheritance, he thought, was probably still virtually certain, and he certainly wouldn't miss the old lady's sad and ridiculous romantic overtures. Without her, perhaps Lori and he could have a normal relationship.

But something was still terribly wrong. He'd catch himself looking at Lori and wondering. He'd seen her doing the same. They suspected each other of murder. That's what it came down to. And if one of them was right? What then?

XXI

Time travel

Alex sat on the steps of the Cyril Benning House, trying to remember exactly how the watercolor looked. Apples maybe. Fruit anyway. A jug of something. All of it on shelves. He'd never paid attention to the label that called it a root cellar. He watched Ms. Mulholland come out of the museum and walk briskly across the grass to the Old Shrubsbury School House Museum gift shop to check the visitors for the day before. Minutes later, she was on her way to where he waited.

"The Sheltons were here."

"Yeah. I was afraid so."

"At least we have some idea of why Aggie was in the root cellar," she said. "I wonder what she thought she was looking for. I wonder if she found it. Apparently, the Sheltons don't think so. They're looking for a high paying customer willing to buy the two works to figure out the secret of the root cellar, and Howe's house."

Alex sighed. "I wish I could squint at the watercolor."

"You wouldn't find any image behind what's there, Alex. Watercolor isn't like that. Maybe that's why he used it instead of oils. He couldn't have put an image over what was already there because what he'd already painted would be washed away when he tried to paint over it."

"So the watercolor was like an official document. There couldn't be anything tricky about it."

"It's like Nate was trying to tell a story, isn't it? I think that's how Aggie understood it. The baby was born; he paints her out. He paints out his house; he obliterates himself. Why? Because the whole thing was shameful and he wanted to cancel it out, especially for Juliette's sake. I think Aggie thought the paintings made up a narrative of what happened, and that the watercolor of the root cellar contained proof of Isabelle's existence. Since we have no record of the baby's birth or death, and we don't know what the root cellar was supposed to have signified, maybe we should try to do something else. Maybe we should try to find out where Howe went after he left Shrubsbury. If he, or someone he knew, was caring for baby Isabelle she should be in the 1840 census."

That evening, Alex looked on eBay for the watercolor. It wasn't there, but a sentence had been added to the description of the landscape: "We are in possession of other Nathan Howe works, for anyone who has a special interest in his art."

Hoping to keep their partnership quiet, the two detectives met next in front of Coker's house where the school bus dropped

Alex along with his friend. Ms. M arrived in a cloud of dust in Adrian Dabney's truck. Poor Mr. Dabney. He'd always kept his truck shiny black. After just a few miles Ms. Mulholland had caked it in gray.

"How'd you get Dab to give you his truck?" Alex asked, as they drove off.

"I told him something was wrong with mine and I wasn't going to be able to get it fixed until tomorrow, that I had a doctor's appointment, and you know at my age how important those medical events are. He had no choice. It was either loan me his truck or expect my imminent demise."

"What's demise?"

"The end. Death."

"Cool."

"Where should I park at your house?"

"We'll put it in the garage. Mom won't be home for more than an hour."

Inside Alex's house, they huddled over his computer. Ms. M watched in amazement as Alex fingered the keys and the screens changed from one color and configuration to another until they ended at Ancestry.com. "Your fingers perform magic, Alex," she murmured, pulling out her credit card. "You're like the child Mozart on the keyboard." They bought their way into the program and began going through 1840 in Vermont and New Hampshire.

They couldn't find Nathan in the 1840 census, but he was with his wife and a six-year-old girl in Concord, New Hampshire, in 1850. The girl was probably the Charlotte of the painting at Grandmother Howe's. There was no Isabelle, and there weren't any other Howes in the same town. The investigation was awesome, thought Alex. It was like time travel, spying on people in the past. Because it was getting late and his mother would be home soon, Ms. Mulholland left him in charge of the investigation. He was her sidekick again. He'd continue the search for Isabelle after he finished his homework.

Alex was excited that night when he found an Isabelle, until he discovered dozens more, many the right age. None of them was named Howe. They married, they had offspring, they became widows, they died.

XXII

How to think about murder

Tasha Mulholland had mixed feelings about taking Alex back as a partner, but it was clear that he'd continue to play detective, with or without her. Maybe their secret partnership would be less dangerous for him. At least, she could keep track of him. She'd complained to everyone who would listen—Adrian, Lori, even Sera—that Alex was busy with soccer and school and that she wasn't seeing much of him. She missed him, but maybe next summer.

Aside from the possible danger, she liked having him back. He was full of ideas and insights. That he'd taken note of the Howe watercolor when no one else had, impressed her. Stuart would never have noticed it, even at his most curious and alert. And certainly not now that he was grown.

But even though she and Alex thought they knew many things they hadn't before, they were far from solving the mystery of Aggie's death, and Tasha Mulholland was as uncertain as ever where Aggie's money should go. She couldn't afford to make any mistakes. In the meantime she worried that they'd been sidetracked by the Howe mystery. Maybe it had nothing to do with the murder or the inheritance.

While Alex was safely in school the next day, she decided to check out the root cellar again, this time slowly, methodically. She didn't tell Stuart; she knew he wouldn't approve. He thought her foolish already, and wanted her to stay away from anything having to do with the murder, though how she could do that and still represent Aggie's concerns she couldn't imagine.

The museum was closed for the day. Adrian was away at a meeting of Vermont museum directors in Montpelier. Not even Lori was around. She was making a presentation of old objects at a nursing home to help elderly residents retrieve their memories of the past. Ms. Mulholland had the museum to herself, and the place was peaceful except for the rattling of an autumn breeze in the rafters and the groaning normal to old buildings on days like this. The yellow police tape was gone. Adrian had prevailed on Stuart to remove it so that the place would seem normal again. All she had to do was unlock the root cellar door with what was clearly not the only key, and study the walls, the corners, and the ceiling of the place with two lanterns and a good flashlight. Simple, except for trying to avoid the dried blood that still encrusted the haphazard crisscross of boards on the dirt floor.

She didn't know what she was looking for, but certainly not an object—that would have been displaced years ago and, if not,

Stuart would have found it. There was no reason to think that the cellar held any secrets except for Aggie's murder. For some reason, she or her killer had opened the door to this black hole. It seemed obvious that they thought something was in it, some kind of answer to Aggie's quest.

Tasha figured that the root cellar might have been under construction about the same time as Howe was painting Juliette or making love to her on the Whittingtons' double bed. It wouldn't have been difficult for him to scribble some mysterious words or numbers on a stone. Or stick something between stones. Even Juliette in her silks could have, though perhaps not without attracting some attention. Tasha couldn't imagine anything else but that sort of graffiti—no buried treasure, no maps to buried treasure.

For half an hour, she peered in corners and under boards, but there was nothing, just big cold granite stones, and not even a space that could have held something except the very smallest something in the chinks between stones. She closed the room and sat by the huge fireplace in an ancient rocker, rocking back and forth. At first, her movement was agitated and the boards in the room responded with groans and squawks. Gradually, the chair quieted. Why not try to imagine the morning of the murder? It shouldn't be that difficult, although it might be uncomfortable, to imagine herself as Aggie encountering her killer.

So she imagined that she was Aggie on that cold cloudy morning when even the moon had disappeared. She was scattered mentally the way Aggie usually was, stumbling a little in the darkness, while the lantern dangling from her hand flashed swaths of light around. She found herself smiling, looking forward to the surprise she'd planned for everybody. She let herself in the kitchen door and locked it behind her. Even though she had a lantern she turned on the overhead bulb in the closet. The building was always eerie when you were alone in it, and especially in the dark. The more light the better.

Of course, light made shadows and Aggie knew the people who used to live here as well as Tasha did, and perhaps even better. Don Carlos Baxter, named, she supposed, after a Spanish king, was helping the cook lay a fire in the kitchen. The dancing light made more shadows. Thankful Smith came in from the barn where she'd finished milking the cow she'd brought with her to school, carrying a pitcher to share with her roommates. Mercy Evensong was dipping water from the cistern catchall and lugging it to the pan where the fire would heat it. One of the students, or was it a teacher, bustled in and murmured something indistinct. The sounds everyone made were as muffled as the shadows were blurred. Mercy and the cook went to open the root cellar door: just a shove would do it.

But what about Aggie? She'd studied the watercolor upstairs. She knew where she wanted to go and why. But she couldn't budge the door—she was old, she was frail. And that was the first question. Presuming that there were no ghosts able or willing to open it, how did Aggie get into the root cellar when the door was so heavy and swollen that two men could only just move it a few hours later? Someone must have helped her.

Any one of the people who came to the museum at Aggie's invitation a few hours later might have helped. Adrian was the most obvious. Tasha wondered if he was on intimate terms with Don Carlos, with Thankful, with Mercy. He certainly had a key, even though he told Stuart he hadn't. So Adrian then. He appeared because Aggie asked him to come let her into the cellar. She glared at him, not for any particular reason, just because she always did. She couldn't help it; she despised him. His attempt to con her with Lori especially rankled. But she wasn't any more afraid of Adrian than of the shadows in the kitchen. Like Tasha Mulholland she might have been suspicious and irritated, but never afraid. So Adrian opened the door and watched as Aggie stepped down into the cellar. She'd already told him something of what she was about, but she wouldn't tell him everything. Eventually, bored and impatient, he left her there. Unless he murdered her first.

Adrian probably left the kitchen door to the outside open. He often did.

Maybe it was Sera who came next. No one knew she was in town. Uninvited, incredulous at her mother's unfeeling welcome, she glared down at her in the root cellar with all the rage she'd inherited growing like a fire in the fireplace until the room was seared with the heat of it. Stabbing Aggie with a bread knife and stowing her in the butter churn might have seemed a perfectly natural thing to do.

What if it was Harold Plumbwell who came instead of

Adrian or Sera? She'd already paid him to do many things for her, why not ask him to open the cellar door? Plumbwell dreamed of proving that he was the descendent she should reward, even though he hadn't yet been quite able to nail down the Isabelle connection. What if she saw something in the root cellar that wasn't to his benefit and laughed at him?

What if it was Lori who came? She was strong enough to have helped push the door open. She could see the girl's anxious face, leaning into the cellar. "Is there anything else I can do?" She wanted Aggie's approval, but all she got was a curt shake of the head. Okay, if that's the way she wanted it, she'd leave her there. So she did. But what if, instead, she began to argue. "I'm your daughter, the only daughter who cares for you." Her voice rose to a near scream.

No matter who killed her, in the name of all that's holy, why would they or anyone else have taken the body out of the root cellar and placed it in the butter churn? There was so much rage in the gesture.

Were there two people—one who killed and one who disposed of the body in the churn?

What if the person who moved the body didn't know who killed her? What if he just found the murdered Aggie and moved her to the churn so she'd be found?

The students went about their business. What was all this to them? Their school was such an unlikely place for a murder. They wouldn't believe it, if they'd seen it, if the blood on the root cellar floor was made visible to them. Shadows on the walls, shadows flitting about the kitchen. They wouldn't have seen a thing.

Someone was muttering at the door, struggling with the lock. Lightning filled the darkening kitchen; thunder rumbled; the sky was about to open up. Ms. Mulholland roused herself and went to open the door. Lori was standing there in a cluster of boxes of egg beaters, rolling pins, fly catchers and a horn to call people to dinner, more, none of it worse for wear after an afternoon's fondling by the elderly denizens of Heavenly Haven Rest Home. An ox yoke was draped around her neck. It had seemed an efficient way to carry it when she unloaded the car.

"Here," said Ms. Mulholland, and carefully lifted the yoke from the girl's shoulders, "let me help you with all that, Lori. My goodness, you took a lot. Did they enjoy your show?"

"I guess. God, I'm tired, Ms. Mulholland. I need a day off."

"Why don't you just leave it all in the closet and put it back in the morning?"

"A good idea. I will."

Helping Lori trundle the boxes to the closet, she found herself alarmed by the girl's appearance. Her hair was damp and splayed out around her pale face like a red nimbus, her eyes wide. She sounded almost querulous. "What are you doing here? You haven't had to give any tours, have you?"

"No, dear," Tasha Mulholland answered. "I just needed to check something in a book upstairs and when I came down again, I couldn't help but sit down and think about Mrs. Hamilton. Odd, even though she was a pain, I miss her terribly."

"Me too," Lori said and her eyes instantly filled with tears.

"You poor dear," said Tasha Mulholland and reached out to hug her without thinking. "I think you really must have cared about her."

"She was my mother, Ms. M. I know no one believed that, including her. But it was true."

Ms. Mulholland did the motherly thing and hugged the girl without thinking much about it, but while she was stroking Lori's hair she had an insight. Something terribly obvious. Of course. The watercolor wasn't a painting of the Old Shrubsbury School House Museum root cellar. It was of Nate Howe's root cellar.

XXIII

Looking for Isabelle

After one of the longest school days Alex had ever known, he bicycled over to Shrubsbury Pond in another effort to keep their sleuthing together a secret, and was skipping stones when Tasha Mulholland pulled up in her very visible yellow truck. She parked it as far under the trees as possible.

She brought a bag full of peanut butter cookies and they munched on them while they sat on a big rock. Canada geese on their way south paraded out on the water. She told him about her ruminations of the day before, and Lori's appearance. "I can't believe she's the murderer. She seems so distraught over Aggie's death."

The past was more frustrating even than the present for a detective. There must be an easier way: another painting to squint at, a diary, a map. "Why is she so sure Mrs. Hamilton was her mother? Mrs. Hamilton didn't think so."

"I'm not sure."

"Maybe she just wants the money. Maybe she knows what

174

you're doing and she's trying to sucker you. You heard her with Nick."

"Yes. But even so, I doubt it. But I had an idea, a really good idea, while I was comforting poor Lori," said Ms. Mulholland, barely containing her excitement.

"What's that, Ms. M?"

"An insight, an illumination. I don't think the root cellar in the watercolor is the one in the Old Shrubsbury School. I think it belonged to Nathan Howe."

Alex laughed out loud. LOL. Of course.

He was ready to run, not drive to Nathan Howe's cellar hole, but Ms. Mulholland slowed him down. With a side arm pitch, she skipped a stone twice across the water. "If there's anything hidden there, Alex, it's not going to be easy to find. It's been falling apart for years, one rock on top of another, dirt covering up more dirt. Let's think before we start shoveling and moving rocks around."

"Think what?" Alex let loose a flatter stone shaped like a missile. It skipped twice.

"Try to remember the watercolor again. There were shelves?"

"Yes."

"And what was on them?"

"Vegetables, fruit. Squash, lettuce, an apple, something else I don't remember...."

"Any jugs or bottles?"

"Yeah. A jug."

"Anything else?"

"I don't think so. It's a small painting. Why?"

"You know that whatever we find won't look at all like the picture. The earth and rocks will have caved in on each other many times. My best guess then is that the jug contained whatever the painting was painted for, probably some legal proof of Isabelle's birth. Or death. My second best guess would be that the carrots and squash tell us that Howe buried whatever it is in his vegetable garden. But that's a bit far-fetched. The problem is that an old lady and a boy aren't going to be able to do all the necessary digging at Howe's house. We have to get some help."

She whipped another stone across the pond and it skipped once, twice, three times. Alex shrugged. His masculine pride was hurt, but what could he do? She was just that good. "Who can we trust?" she asked.

That was how Coker came to be involved. Add two boys together—especially when one is over-sized—and you get one man. Ms. M hadn't any better idea.

It was Saturday morning when Ms. Mulholland and the boys hiked up to the cellar hole. She'd told Stuart, Adrian, even Sera Hamilton, that they were going berry picking and doing a nature walk in preparation for a nature study on Monday's Fall Harvest Day, a yearly museum get-together of kids from all over the county.

When they got to the site the three of them sat on the stones that had been Nathan Howe's foundation, and talked about the house and what it must have looked like.

"It probably faced the road, don't you think, Ms. M?" said Alex.

"Probably," she answered. "You remember the little house in the painting at Grandma Howe's?"

"It can't be the same house."

"No. But if he built both of them, he probably did it in pretty much the same way. Remember there was a porch open on two sides. He could sit on the porch and look down at Juliette's house."

"Hey," said Coker, who was almost as smart as Alex, "so the porch probably ran from there to there, or maybe not quite that long, because it looks like the foundation ends here, and a porch would have fronted it and wouldn't have had a foundation."

"Good thinking, Coker," said Ms. M.

The two boys tried to find a continuous wall around the hole, but it was hard to identify when everything was filled in with earth and bramble. "Anyway, the back of the house is right up here," said Alex, poking around with a stick on the other side of a wall of stone. "Doesn't it seem like the root cellar might have been over here somewhere?"

"Might have been," agreed Ms. M. "It must have been close to the house or under the house so there'd be easy access in the winter. But that still leaves us with too much space to just dig. Were the walls made of stone or wood on the watercolor, Alex?"

"The painting was so dark I'm not sure."

"If they were wood, they would have rotted out a long time ago."

"Do you think this is why Aggie wanted an archaeological dig?"

"Absolutely. I think she may have guessed the root cellar might be here instead of at the museum. She never got the chance to explore that notion."

They figured that the garden might have been just beyond where the root cellar was, but the whole area was a tangle of blackberry bramble. While the boys hacked away at the bush and looked for clues, Ms. M sat and stared at the stones, thinking about the painting. "Alex, Coker," she said finally. "He probably made a very simple root cellar. After all, he may not have thought he would stay long. He was an itinerant painter. What if there was a cave of rocks in that embankment there—or if he created one? Most of it may be gone, but look, maybe this is part of it." She pointed her shovel at the bank, poking at something that was punky and could once have been wood.

"When Nathan got ready to stash something important, he would have wanted to put it in a place that would last a long time. Maybe longer than his house. I doubt he thought about one hundred and sixty-five years, but nonetheless—" She pulled aside some brush, and cut some more. She seemed to have a particular place in mind, as if she'd looked for root cellars many times, and knew just where to find one made 165 years ago. The three of them dug silently for over an hour. Alex wailed in despair now and again, but no one stopped. "If it isn't here, Alex, I'm not sure what else we can do."

Every once in a while, there was a sound like footsteps—breaking twigs, shuffling rocks—but it was no one, just the wind in the trees, a squirrel on a high branch, a skunk, a porcupine, a raccoon. Still, they hid the shovels and clippers when they broke for lunch. When they actually heard human feet, boots they thought, coming up the hill through the trees, it was a simple matter to gather up the water bottles and sandwiches and duck down on the other side of the oak remains in the middle of the lilac bush.

Alex expected Principal Plumbwell; Ms. Mulholland was looking for Nick Crafts. They were surprised to see Adrian Dabney. He sat down on the same stone Ms. Mulholland and Alex had shared a minute earlier, and pulled a picture out of a canvas case. He stared at it, then looked up and around. He repeated the same action several times, each time looking somewhere else, before he stopped, frowned, and then did it again. Ms. Mulholland caught her breath: did he see the brush that had been disturbed by their feet? He was likely to guess that someone else was here, and soon. She turned to Alex and Coker who were wide-eyed and motionless, put a finger to her lips to shush them, then silently mouthed the words: "Stay here. Stay hidden. When we've gone, follow us down the hill and call Stuart." Alex nodded. She silently prayed he understood every word of her instruction, and walked out onto the floor of the cellar hole.

"Hello, Adrian."

Adrian Dabney jumped and the blood drained from his face until he was white as white paper. "Hello, Tasha. What are you doing here?" he squeaked.

"I might ask you the same question. What's the picture?"

"Oh, it's just an old watercolor."

"By Nathan Howe. And you've brought it to the site of his house. But I think it belongs in the Shrubsbury Room."

"Yes. I just borrowed it. You know how we've always thought it was of the root cellar in the museum? It just occurred to me that it could as well have pictured Nathan Howe's cellar."

"You borrowed it? From the Sheltons?"

"I don't know what you're talking about." He put the picture down on a stone as if it was inconsequential. His hands went limp and dangled helplessly.

"I wonder. I don't know how much you do know. Tell me what you're really doing here, Adrian. You know that after one hundred and sixty-five years there's not going to be a root cellar here."

"I'll bet I don't know nearly as much as you think I do. Aggie told me that there was a narrative of events in Nathan Howe's paintings, events that had to do with a forgotten baby and another better heir to her fortune than Sera. And to her house, of course. So much for my dreams of adding the house to the museum and spending some of her capital where it should have been spent years ago. She just laughed at me about it."

"When did she tell you this?"

"The day before her murder, when she invited me to her early morning lecture, to her murder as it turned out." He held up his right hand. "Swear on the Bible, the flag, whatever you want, that's when it happened." He nervously tapped his fingers on his leg. "Anyway, she told me about the baby in the portrait of Juliette; I knew there was a painting of the road up this hill from almost the same date even though she didn't describe it. Aggie didn't say anything about the watercolor. It's such a silly little painting, I'd forgotten it existed. There's no root cellar at the Hamilton House, although I suppose there must have been one back then. Of course, there's nothing left here."

"And what did you think you'd find in a root cellar that may be only barely here?" Ms. Mulholland picked up the painting and sat down next to him. She wasn't afraid of him at all, thought Alex. She doesn't think he killed Aggie. Why not? She had always been able to read Adrian Dabney, and she'd always seemed to like him. To Alex he was a ridiculous figure; he didn't understand him at all, and that meant he might be guilty of almost anything.

"You're the executrix, aren't you? Aggie's executrix?"

"Yes."

"I thought so. I don't know. I imagine Aggie was looking for proof that Juliette had a daughter. I don't know whether she had any information about the baby's later life. Or whether she knew who the distant cousin was that she might leave her fortune to. But first things first. She at least knew there was a daughter. I guess the father must have been the painter Howe."

"Seems that way."

He looked around, his eyes clouding as his mind boggled at the task that lay before him. "We'll need some honest-to-God archaeologists to uncover anything here."

Ms. Mulholland stared down at the little canvas for a few minutes.

"Can you make anything of it, Tasha?"

"I honestly can't. I don't know what it means. It's an odd subject for a painter, especially an American primitive. Not a conventional still life in the European sense. I don't think I've ever seen another like it. And of course the date is the same as on the two oil paintings. Why would he have painted it unless he meant it to say something? To add to the narrative, so to speak? What's fascinating is that the cellar had stone walls and, I think, a stone floor."

"What do you think? Could you think of an excuse for a grant and some archaeologists to dig? Write a proposal?"

"Yes, but not soon enough. The will has to be settled in another two and a half weeks. But there must be a way. Let's go sit somewhere comfortable and see if we can come up with something."

"I'd like that. It's hot and dirty here, and I don't feel the least inspired."

Coker rolled his eyes at Alex. Hot, huh. Not inspired. Perspiration rolled down his chubby face, making brown marks like branches on a weeping tree. He moved just a little, shifting his weight, shaking his head. Then his eyes popped open wide. He pointed down at the ground and nudged Alex once, twice, again and again.

"One question, Adrian. If there was obvious evidence of a legitimate heir somewhere here, what would you have done with it?"

"Honestly? If I hadn't run into the executrix, if I'd found that kind of proof, I'd have destroyed it. Sera would be grateful. Something could be worked out. But I've run into you, and I know enough about you to know that option is closed to me. So, the answer for the public and posterity is, I don't know."

"We'll talk more about that too." As they started walking down the hill, Alex stood up silently, waiting, eager to run after them, waiting to pursue them when they were far enough away and he could be almost as silent as an Indian in moccasins, while Coker stayed and phoned Stuart on his cell phone. He didn't want to let Ms. Mulholland out of his sight. He didn't trust Adrian even a little. But Coker was down on the ground, wiggling around.

"Hey, Alex. I've found something," he hissed.

Alex kneeled back down. "Jeeze, Coker. Not now. What?"

"It's a dish maybe."

"It's part of a jug." Alex recognized the thick gray stoneware with the cobalt blue vines, like the jug in the watercolor. "Mark the spot. We have to save Ms. Mulholland."

Coker fired up his phone, while Alex followed Adrian Dabney and Ms. Mulholland, staying well behind them. Adrian wasn't good at walking downhill in the woods and even though Ms. Mulholland might not be all that agile, she could move a lot faster than the museum director. He almost laughed out loud watching her politely trying to let Adrian Dabney help her when a sudden dip or a bank of heavy undergrowth blocked the path. Stuart Mulholland would do better to protect Dabney from Ms. M; the Sheriff's mother could take care of herself. Nevertheless, Alex stayed behind them, just in case Dab had a weapon, maybe another bread knife.

The sheriff was waiting at the base of the hill when the two appeared. Alex watched..

"Hi, Mom. Are you all right?"

"I'm fine, Stuart. But I think you, Adrian and I should have a talk. What do you think, Adrian? Let's go to your office."

Alex watched the three walk down the road together for a few minutes, and then headed back up the hill where he met Coker skittering down. "Let's go dig some more. The stone cellar in the picture had a stone floor and stone walls. And that jug—maybe the jug is the one in the painting."

"Hey, yeah," said Coker, smiling cheerfully. His blisters had stopped hurting. He'd found the first real clue and even though he didn't quite understand what they were looking for, he felt important.

Ten minutes after the boys began shoveling again, they found another shard of crockery. A half hour later, sweaty and dirty, Coker, his round face a mask of brown dust, sat down on everyone's favorite stone and swore he'd stop working unless Alex told him everything. Alex would probably have complied, but someone was breaking through the bush below. In a rush, they covered the holes they'd dug with the same brush they used earlier to hide from Adrian, and crouched down further away in the lilac, spades at the ready. They clutched them more tightly when they saw who it was. Principal Harold Plumbwell, red-faced and breathless, a bottle of water grasped in one hand, stood at the edge of the cellar hole, staring into it. Television-inspired fantasies of killing or being killed by the man ran through Alex's mind. And a moral dilemma. If he had to, could he hit his hated principal with a shovel? It wouldn't be a good idea to hit him too hard. Somehow, killing a principal seemed more serious than killing other people, something like doing in a policeman. A capital crime—especially if he was your principal.

Plumbwell walked around the site for a few minutes, glancing at the space where the boys had been digging but apparently not seeing anything amiss, then sitting down for a full five minutes, wiping his perspiring brow, catching his breath, drinking from his bottle of water. Finally, he walked over to a wall of field stones on the far side of the hole, as if he'd been here many times before and knew exactly what he was doing. He knelt down and took a small object out of a space between the rocks, then pushed it into the wall a little higher up to make it more visible. When he stood up again, his knees cracked and Coker barely held back a giggle. Plumbwell peered in their direction and started to walk over to make sure no one was there, but seeing no one, he stopped short, and scuffed out any knee or footprints he'd left in the dusty floor of the cellar hole. The boys held their breath and waited. He combed his oily hair back with his fingers, tucked his shirt back into his pants, looked over again towards the place the boys were hidden, and started back down the hill. Alex and Coker squeezed hands and struggled against the laughs that were growing in their throats. Somehow, they stayed still until the man's footsteps were muffled by distance, and then even until they heard his car start up.

"Christ! That was close! We were almost goners, Coker. Snuffed out by our own principal!"

Coker was on the ground laughing. "Bummer Plumber! Oh, God."

"We should have heard him coming. Not good, Coker. Not professional at all. He parked at the church. I just thought, well, that's it. Dabney did it. I never even kept watch for anyone else."

"It's okay. He didn't know we were here. Oh, God. I can't believe it. Bummer Plumber." He started laughing all over again, and Alex joined him.

When they stopped laughing, Coker was the first to ask: "So what did he leave in the stone wall, Alex? Let's go look."

Alex shook his head. "I don't think so. It's evidence, and we don't even have gloves. He may have left his fingerprints on it. We're just kids. No one's going to believe us if we say we saw him leave it. But the fingerprints will convince them. We have to wait for Ms. M. She'll know what to do and how to do it."

"You and Ms. M are trying to find Old Aggie's murderer, aren't you, Alex? That's what this is all about, isn't it? Jeeze. Do you think Plumbwell did it?"

"I don't know," Alex said, feeling confused and light-headed and wishing devoutly that his partner would return.

Adrian Dabney sighed with relief when Ms. Mulholland and her tiresome son finally left. He'd always liked Ms. M but her interference in his efforts to make money for the museum was annoying. It was hard enough to raise the funds to keep everything going. It was a shame that money was what was needed because he really didn't like money. Or even power, for that matter. His disdain for material things in a world mad for them set him apart. In his own way, he was pure, and proud of it.

As a boy, he was teased unmercifully by other children—and worse, by his own family. He was a runt of a kid with bad eyes and a voice that had an inner whine, as if it were the mechanism in his throat that drove his every utterance. His physical deficiencies shaped his personality, so that even when he grew up and, for a decade or two, achieved a look that attracted women looking for intellectual men who were sensitive, there was something unhealthy in his personality that kept them from fully embracing him. He'd been divorced by two wives, and left behind by three children.

What most annoyed others was his assumption of his own superiority. That, in combination with a terrible need for everyone's good opinion and what was turning into a lifelong quest for money and free stuff for the museum, had made him almost unbearably ingratiating. He was perpetually the kid in Dickens' *Oliver Twist* with his hand out, begging for "more."

Adrian put his feet up on his desk, and gazed out at the

museum building. He remembered when he discovered history, the present faded to past, captured in books, pictures, artifacts and artifice. He was seven years old when he first visited the Old Shrubsbury School House Museum with his class from school. It was like a giant doll house filled with a collection of old things, the past condensed and labeled. What he feared, and that was nearly everything, had been tamed by time and turned into something that could be memorized, written down, collected and interpreted. He only had to wait and the scary present, and even scarier future, passed into history, and he was in charge. In the museum, he found a domain he could dominate and control, if only the money to keep it all going wasn't so hard to find.

Agatha Hamilton had been a problem for most of the years he'd been in Shrubsbury. Now, even in death, she stymied him. A sizeable portion of her fortune rightfully belonged to the museum, if only because she took so much from it. It might not happen immediately, but Adrian Dabney knew with self-certainty that he'd find a way to get Aggie's money, despite Ms. M and her son. He gritted his teeth, remembering his struggle over the years and still today. His neck stiffened and reddened. His small eyes glazed over. He'd do whatever it took, no matter what that meant.

XXIV

Finding Isabelle

By the time Ms. Mulholland finished her interview with Adrian Dabney and saw her son, the sheriff, off to the softball game between the sheriff's department and the volunteer firemen that had been interrupted by Coker's call (who, he asked, was the kid on the phone anyway?), by the time she climbed back up the hill, the boys were dutifully but not very happily digging again. "Hey, Ms. M, we thought you'd never get back. Wait 'til we tell you what happened! Did you get Dabney sorted out? Do you think he did the murder?"

Ms. Mulholland hadn't learned much from Adrian about his actions before and since Aggie's death. He'd been trying to stall her attempt to read the narrative in Nathan Howe's paintings and find a lost ancestor. After her death he'd worked with the Major to keep the narrative from being found out by anyone else, especially her executrix. But he had nothing to do with her death, he said. He might be a scoundrel, but he was no killer. He repeated his denial over and over in a singsong voice as if it were a mantra.

189

While she was gone the boys had found part of the jug in the painting. At least it looked like the same jug. Amazing and wonderful! And Principal Plumbwell? They'd done well to keep quiet, to control themselves, to wait for gloves to look at what the man had placed in the cranny of the wall. And yes, she had gloves, she always had white cotton gloves in her pocket.

The boys found the cranny for her. "I wonder why he thought the root cellar would be here," she said, as she pulled a metal canister out from the wall. "Does he know something we don't? Or was he just guessing? Clearly, he wanted this to be found."

"Oh yeah."

Ms. Mulholland carefully pulled the stopper out of the metal container. Inside was a rolled piece of paper—stiff, yellowing, fragile, but apparently intact. She unrolled it far enough for them to make out what it was, afraid to flatten it any further and break up the parchment. It seemed to be Isabelle's baptismal certificate.

"Does it look legit?"

"It certainly looks it. But we need an expert's opinion."

"Why would he have stashed it here? How did he find it to begin with?"

"I don't know. I truly don't know, Alex, but I suspect the existence of Isabelle is supposed to support his claim to Aggie's house and fortune."

"You think it's a con, Ms. Mulholland?" asked Coker.

"We'll have it examined. The last evidence we have suggests that Mrs. Hamilton thought Plumbwell's genealogy was unlikely to be legitimate. I don't think Aggie wanted him to be an heir. I know I don't."

"I hope he's a con man and we find it out," Alex said..

"Fellows, I have a favor to ask you. I'd like us to dig a little more. If he is conning us, then there may still be something here. Those bits of jug are a good sign."

Both boys groaned.

"Let's see what you've done so far." They walked over to the hole in the ground the boys had made. Ms. Mulholland picked up a shovel and tapped around in the same area. "The root cellar probably caved in completely, but even if it did, the ground might be less dense where it was, there might be more rotted wood from the shelf, more air."

"Jeeze, Ms. M, Plumbwell seemed to know where it was and it wasn't out here!" said Alex, feeling irritable. He was tired. She hadn't been digging forever and ever. Let her do it if she wanted it done.

Ms. Mulholland took her shovel and thrust it into a mess of rocks, then began working around each rock she found, catching it under her spade, pulling it out, tossing it aside. "We're also looking for a rock bottom. In the painting it looks as if there may have been several flat rocks pieced together like a jigsaw puzzle." Alex sighed. He and Coker began digging with her.

It wasn't long before they found another smaller piece of jug. "If Nate put something into the jug and it's broken, don't you think the something will have putrefied away by now?"

"It depends on the something."

Ms. M and the two boys dug in silence for a while, tossing more and more rocks to one side, discovering still another shard of the jug, and then striking metal. It was another smaller metal box, little enough to fit in a jug, and mashed in the middle by rocks and the years. It was corroded shut and they had to wait to jimmy it open until they got back to Ms. Mulholland's for milk and Oreos. (She hadn't had time to bake.)

The boys ran back to Ms. M's apartment; she walked. A half hour passed before they were finally at the table together. She outfitted them with cotton gloves. Alex pulled out the paper this time. It wasn't quite as yellowed or stiff as the first one which made Ms. Mulholland wonder if Plumbwell's document was more recently made. Something else in the box slid out and clattered to the table. A small round copper-colored locket. Alex looked at it gravely.

"Shall I open it, Ms. M?"

"Today, there'd be a photograph inside. It'll be interesting to see what Nathan Howe put in an 1830's locket."

Alex pried it open with his nails. He whistled softly, "It's a baby's hair, isn't it? I think she died."

Ms. Mulholland carefully opened the paper, a death certificate; Isabelle lived less than three months. So much for Grandma Howe's story, so much for Plumbwell's genealogy, so much for Alex's Isabelle. Nathan Howe was memorializing his love affair and his daughter, not providing clues to an inheritance. At first Alex was disappointed, but then he was glad. Nate was a good guy; he wasn't like Alex's father at all.

XXV

Con men

Tasha Mulholland was pleased that Principal Plumbwell had almost certainly been eliminated as an heir. And more good had come from finding him and Adrian out. There were no new bids on the remaining painting on Shelton's website. Adrian had covered for the Sheltons in front of her and Stuart, but if they dreamed of a higher profit, they were about to be disappointed. She'd driven to her son's home that evening, rousted him from the living room sofa and the first quarter of a football game, then gone with him to the Sheriff's Department to put the evidence where it couldn't be stolen or lost. He promised to send it out the next morning to someone in Montpelier who could authenticate both the papers and the tin boxes that contained them. If the death certificate was genuine, Harold Plumbwell and Nick Crafts would both be out of the running. Soon she'd know who should inherit and her job would be finished. Or at least that job. She was no closer to knowing who killed Aggie. In fact, she felt as if she were further from that truth than ever. All she'd got for her trouble were more questions: Had Aggie discovered Plumbwell's con and had he silenced her? Did Adrian kill her so that she wouldn't give all her money to Plumbwell? Or Crafts? Maybe, just maybe, Sera was the most likely killer of all.

It was an early Sunday afternoon and Ms. Mulholland was spinning in front of the barn. Alex was off playing soccer, so she had time to think while she spun but, like the spinning wheel, all she could do was go round in circles. She'd been through all of it so many times. When Nick Crafts drove up, she was relieved. She could stop thinking and just do her usual clever and convivial old lady thing. Nick was, she thought, the easiest of the suspects to lie to.

"Hallo," he said, climbing out of his truck.

"Hello, Nick. It's good to see you."

"It's good to see you, Tasha. I have a question for you."

"I hope I can answer it."

"I just came from the cellar hole on the hill. It looks like someone's been hanging there and digging. Do you know anything about it? I know I haven't bought the property yet but I'm really curious and a little worried."

"It's all right, Nick. Your cellar hole was the home to a mystery that's since been solved. Adrian and I talked about your archaeological dig, and we're all for it by the way. We won't do any more experimental digs there without expert help."

"What mystery?" There was an edge in his voice.

"Howe's old cellar hole contained evidence that Juliette

Whittington, the resident of the Hamilton House when Howe was painting her, had given birth to a baby and that Howe was probably the father instead of Gerald Whittington, Juliette's husband."

"My God, whole novels are happening and I don't know anything about them. Tell me everything, Tasha, please."

What she told him was enough and no more. She implied that the boys dug because she made them, and weren't really very interested in the place or its stories. She had to protect them no matter how ridiculous it seemed. She didn't mention that Plumbwell planted the evidence of Isabelle's existence; in fact, she didn't say a word about the man. Nick may already have known it if Plumbwell was working with him. She told him that Adrian spent some time looking at the cellar hole, but not that he'd been trying to sabotage Aggie's search for an heir. And she didn't mention the death certificate. She looked forward to surprising all of them with that. She watched Nick's face closely as she talked and when she was through, she understood that, like her, he knew things he wasn't telling.

"Why are you concerned about Howe's affair and Howe's daughter? I mean it's a good story, and I can tell you like good stories, but I'm surprised you spent an afternoon digging for one."

"The boys are doing archaeology, and it seemed like a logical place to do a little digging, especially since there was a mystery about the baby who reappeared in Howe's painting. Gave the dig a purpose and a soupçon of excitement, if you know what I mean."

Nick laughed. "Yeah. I do. It's kind of cool, all of it. So

who's likely to inherit my cellar hole at this point, Ms. M?"

"I honestly don't know. Despite the baptismal certificate, I still think the most obvious candidate is Aggie's daughter, Sera."

"Yeah. I guess so, huh?" He studied his feet uneasily, self-consciously, then glanced at his watch, and got up from the grass where he'd been sitting. "I'm sorry, Tasha. I'd rather stay and talk, but I promised someone that I'd stop by the soccer game, and I see I'm late already."

Ms. M realized again that she really couldn't trust anyone anymore, except Alex, and she'd better get used to it. Nick was as charming as ever, but she knew more about him now.

Plumbwell would probably be by later in the day, after the soccer game. He didn't know it yet, but he was in for a shock and she wanted to be the one to tell him. His supposed ancestor probably died long ago, and the little man had no recourse but to dissemble and hope to get away sooner rather than later. While she sat there thinking about him, the villainous principal drove up—apparently the Shrubsbury Elementary team had already lost—and leaned out his car window. "Tasha, may I talk with you a minute, please?"

"Of course, Harold." He parked and walked over to where she was working, looked down at her and twirled his pencil thin mustache like an old movie malefactor, all the time smiling his snide smile. "I just heard a rumor. I heard that you and the boys were digging at the Howe cellar hole and found evidence that helps establish that there was a baby born to Agatha Hamilton's ancestor."

"Where did you hear that?"

"It's not true? Nick said you were all up there digging yesterday." So Plumbwell and Nick were in cahoots.

"No, it's true. The boys found a baptismal certificate for Isabelle Whittington, who was actually the illegitimate baby of the artist Nathan Howe."

"Amazing. After all these years."

She couldn't help herself. Plumbwell deserved the full story. "But they also found a death certificate for the infant."

His face reddened. "And where did that come from?" he growled, then tried to recover himself and look merely curious.

"Both certificates seem legitimate. The second one is a real find. The boys dug it up along with some shards of a stoneware jug. Anyway, the sheriff has both of them and they're on their way to a lab where their authenticity can be confirmed."

"That's good. That's very good. A reputable lab, I hope."

"Oh, yes. The best in the state."

"So my claim has probably been shot all to hell."

"If you claim to be related to Isabelle Howe, or Whittington, yes. You could put it that way."

"Well, here's more for you, you old busybody. Aggie had that baptismal certificate made. I was her errand boy, her henchman. She wanted to make her golden boy her heir. I wasn't going to inherit. She let me know from the get-go that she discounted my little genealogy. After she was murdered, I thought I'd try to pull the scam anyway. But Nick was always the man she had in mind and you can bet he's going to be just a little bit disappointed. I can hardly wait to tell him."

"Nick Crafts. You're saying that Aggie paid you to help her establish evidence favoring Nick?"

"Yeah. Cute, huh? I stayed around hoping for a way to flip the situation and get rid of Crafts. But he was her boy." He squeezed out a nasty laugh. "She's had us all trying to out-scheme, out-manipulate, out-perform one another. She enjoyed every minute. I think she hoped someone would get killed, but surprise, surprise."

"It sounds as if you had motive to kill her, Harold. Did you?"

"I should have done it, I almost wish I had. But I didn't." He turned around and walked back to his car, got in and slammed the car door, turned on the motor, and looked over at her with a bemused expression. "Of course, the death certificate could be phony too. I didn't plant it, but someone may have."

"My goodness, your principal is a nasty man," Tasha Mulholland said to Alex when his mother dropped him off after picking him up at the soccer game.

"We lost again, Ms. M," he interrupted, sinking down onto the ground next to the spinning wheel. "And I was one of the worst. I didn't get anywhere near a score. I have flat feet just like my father. I'm a total loser."

"Not by my lights. You're a great detective, and a number one archaeologist besides. I've watched you play, Alexander Churchill. It's not flat feet; it's a matter of focus. You get bored and forget to watch the ball. In time you'll be an excellent soccer player. I know these things. Believe me." He looked at her ruefully. Such a kind old lady, he thought.

She told him about her conversations with Crafts and Plumbwell, editing out the ugliest parts with the schoolmaster.

"So he said that Old Aggie was playing everyone, huh? Do you believe him, Ms. Mulholland?"

"I'm afraid I do, Alex. But even so, I must insist you not call her Old Aggie."

Alex grinned. "Yes, ma'am." Just like her. The old lady turned out to be a scheming, conniving bitch, and Ms. Mulholland still insisted that everyone be polite to her. Dead and all. "So what are we going to do next?"

"I'm not sure. I've spun and spun and I still can't think straight. I think authenticating the documents will solve the problem of the proper heir and I can finish playing executrix. I hope so. But we still haven't any real evidence as to who murdered Aggie, and I can't think how to find any. I wonder sometimes if even the Sheltons had a motive, though I can't think what it would be. Since we have no forensic evidence, how are we to prove or disprove anything?"

"I've been thinking about that. In fact, I was thinking about it when the ball finally came my way," he grinned. "We have to trick the murderer. That's what they do on TV—they trick the murderer into owning up to the murder."

"Who does?"

"The detectives on TV."

Ms. Mulholland nodded thoughtfully. "So, for example, we manufacture some evidence and let everyone know it exists. Mrs. Hamilton's killer hears of it and acts out in some way to destroy it. We spring the trap; they're caught."

"Yeah. Do you have any cookies, Ms. M?"

Elaine Magalis

XXVI

Happy birthday, Timothy Evensong

Monday was Fall Harvest Day. Children wandered from place to place on the museum grounds, their chatter a fantasia of pipes and bells in the bright fall day, their energy flattening the grass and stirring up the oak trees in front of the museum so that acorns rained down on them. Sheep and goats bawled in conversation; the blacksmith's hammer twanged; pens of chickens squawked; horses at the head of a hay wagon neighed as the wheels rumbled down the broad dusty road past the Old Shrubsbury School House. Dozens of children, ages eight to thirteen, came every spring for Spring Field Day and every autumn for Fall Harvest Day to learn about the past of the Northeast Kingdom of Vermont and agricultural America. This year there was a plan afoot to celebrate Timothy Evensong's birthday at the end with a march, a song and a newspaper reporter to counter recent rumors of museum murder and mayhem.

Several murder suspects were in attendance on this extraordinary Fall Harvest Day. Lori Chickering and Adrian

202

Dabney were supervising the affair, running from place to place orienting students and consulting with teachers; Nick Crafts was pressing apples in the cider press; Sera Hamilton, who grew up in Shrubsbury making pots, was demonstrating the use of the pottery wheel; and Principal Plumbwell, smiling his uncomfortably eerie smile, was guardian to two classes of Shrubsbury Elementary School students.

Alex had been drafted to assist Ms. Mulholland in registering students. He was also her gofer for the day. He'd come early and while they set up the registration table together, he and Ms. M discussed the investigation and set their plans in motion. The trap was to be sprung at noon by the plant of a rumor that a student from Irasburg, touring the museum kitchen, had discovered evidence about the murder that no one else had spotted—perhaps a button, a scarf... who knew?— it had just mysteriously materialized in the middle of the collection of butter molds. The Old Shrubsbury School House building, the rumor continued, was off limits for everyone the rest of the day since the sheriff was out of town on an emergency police call and would be unable to collect the new evidence until later.

At noon Sheriff Stuart Mulholland was actually sitting in the gallery next to the kitchen, peering through the interior window at the kitchen. He had agreed to the plan reluctantly. It wasn't an approach to crime he'd used before and he'd certainly never studied it at the police academy. His mother convinced him that this would be his best chance to break the case. Besides, she'd pointed out, nothing would be lost if none of the suspects came to retrieve the evidence. No one knew he was there. They thought he was out helping to bust a marijuana farm on the bay side of Newport City.

At the exact time agreed upon, Alex and Coker made their rounds. Coker took aside a Shrubsbury chatterbox, a seventh-grade girl who was with the rest of her class watching Nick Crafts throw apples into the press and grind them to juice. By the time half the students joined him in turning the handle and mashing the tart green McIntosh apples, the story might as well have been written on a banner and waved in Nick's face. As it was, he registered some alarm, but he didn't leave his station. He just handed out more paper cups.

About the same time, Alex joined a group of Shrubsbury sixth-graders who were building a fence. Principal Harold Plumbwell was just pounding in a stake when he heard the rumor, and stopped mid-stroke to consider what he should do next, if anything.

Alex and Coker joined up to mingle with a group of Orleans students, their competition in their last soccer match. Two of the boys were the most excitable fellows they'd ever met, guys who could not be ignored, especially when they were fired up dancing around the center pole in a tent full of crockery. Sera Hamilton stopped turning a pot and stared at them, overhearing, disbelieving.

Ms. Mulholland was talking with Adrian and Lori in the tea room at the museum's offices, telling them, breathlessly, that a student from Irasburg had made a discovery that could solve Agatha Hamilton's murder. Among the butter paddles and next to the knives, was something they were certain belonged to the murderer. She'd called her son, the sheriff, who was on a Newport drug bust, about the discovery and he'd instructed her to close down the building, and to keep everyone, including herself and the museum's administration outside, until he could get there. It might take him an hour or two to arrive. "What?" queried Adrian. "Are you sure that it's really a clue and not something left at another time?"

"We think it's a clue, Stuart and I," said Ms. Mulholland. "I can't say anything more. It wouldn't be fair to the person who's being implicated since we don't know for sure."

"Well, if it might be nothing," said Lori, "do you think it's fair to turn this into a big deal? Can't we keep the clue safe here while the kids finish their tours of the building?"

"No, Lori. We can't do it that way. We're all under suspicion. The clue must stay where it is, where it was found. There are only two more groups scheduled to tour the museum. They can wait until another time."

"I'm sure you're right," said Adrian. "But what a bother. Have you already shut down the building, or would you like me to go over and make sure it's secure?"

"I can do it," said Lori. "I'd be glad to do it. Then you can finish those figures for the month's financial report."

"Neither of you has to do it," said Tasha Mulholland. "It's

already done."

The coconspirators met back at the education center where the students were gathering for lunch, stilt races, a few fast games of graces, and a marbles tournament. There were cheers and boos, and chaos everywhere. They saw Nick Crafts and the last of his cider-makers setting out a row of jugs of cider; they saw Principal Plumbwell scolding someone who'd just stumbled over him on a pair of stilts; Sera Hamilton was frantically boxing up her pottery, afraid that someone would break something, especially since a liberated hog was racing for her tent with a host of children coming after. Adrian arrived to help quell the pandemonium. By the time the band arrived to lead a parade of children around the museum, Alex, Coker and Ms. Mulholland knew exactly who among the murder suspects was missing.

Inside the museum, Stuart Mulholland waited impatiently. What a crock, he thought to himself. How did he let himself be talked into this idiocy? No one would come; the scheme was too transparent. His legs were cramped from sitting still in the cold building; he would have rather been outside with the kids, helping judge a game of nine pins or showing them how to effectively land a ringer every time in horseshoes. He was surprised when he heard a key turn in the kitchen door and scurrying footsteps in the kitchen. He expected to see his mother with a wan, embarrassed smile on her face: "I'm sorry, Stuart. You were right. It was a lame-brained scheme." He stood up and looked through the interior window. Lori Chickering was anxiously searching through the paddles.

"Miss Chickering," he said.

"Sheriff Mulholland," she replied. Her eyes began to flood with tears.

"What are you looking for Miss?"

"It's not what it looks like. I didn't do it. I didn't kill her. I couldn't have killed her. She was my mother."

Mulholland walked quietly around to the kitchen, handcuffs dangling from one hand, his face stiff and unyielding with the expression he'd been taught to use at the Police Academy. "You're under arrest, Miss Chickering," he said and began to recite the Miranda warning, but before he got halfway into it, she started sobbing uncontrollably. She turned limp. She fainted in a heap at his feet.

If a guilty party was discovered, Sheriff Mulholland had planned to take him or her quietly while the games and festivities continued on the green, and before everyone encircled the museum to sing "Happy Birthday" to Timothy Evensong. Now, he didn't know what to do. He hadn't brought any police assistance with him because he'd been so sure the whole thing would turn out to be a farce, and he didn't want to embarrass himself in front of his deputies. He stood for a moment, confused, then collected a chair and cuffed Lori to one leg while he went to find help. His mother, Alex and Coker were at the kitchen door before he could look for them.

"She fainted, Mom," he said helplessly.

Outside, more than one hundred youngsters were beginning

to gather for their march around the museum. They were moving more quickly than anyone had imagined they would to join hands and circle the building. Sheriff Mulholland would either have to wait to take Lori out or escort his weeping suspect through a hoard of curious, chattering children.

"Coker, you have a bottle of water, don't you?"

Coker smiled broadly, proud that his water could be put to official use, and unhooked the bottle from his belt.

"Alex, Stuart, one of you. Go to the closet. There are some clean dust rags on the top shelf. Bring one."

Alex was there and back in moments. Ms. Mulholland soaked the rag, a checkered dishcloth she'd once used to dry her own dishes, and applied it to Lori's forehead. Gradually, the girl stirred. "I didn't, I didn't do it," she murmured. "I didn't, Tasha. I really didn't."

"Come on, young lady," said Stuart Mulholland in his most professional voice. "You're under arrest on suspicion of the murder of Agatha Hamilton. We'll talk at the station." He and his mother helped her to her feet, and he half dragged the weeping girl to the door. "She was like a mother to me," she wailed again. Outside the children had formed an enormous circle around the house and were marching to the tune of "Yankee Doodle Dandy" played on a tuba, a trumpet and a bass drum. Lori stared out the window, wide-eyed and terrified.

"If you didn't do it, why did you come looking for the incriminating evidence, Lori?" asked Ms. Mulholland gently.

"I was afraid you'd all think I had killed her."

Stuart Mulholland shook his head. "That's not very convincing, Ms. Chickering."

"Happy birthday, Reverend Evensong, happy birthday, Reverend (some of them added rapid fire Timothys), Happy birthday, dear Reverend Evensong. Happy birthday to you." They cheered, they clapped and they began to move out, friends finding friends and heading for the school buses lining the road. Lori and her accusers stood at the door, waiting, not saying anything now since there didn't seem to be more to say.

"Alex, Coker," Ms. Mulholland murmured as the grounds emptied, "You'd better go or Principal Plumbwell will have a fit."

"I don't care if he does," Alex said defiantly, but the expression on her face told him he'd better do as she said. The boys took one last gander at Lori, wondering how such a weepy girl could have killed anyone so brutally, even Old Aggie. Then they slipped out the kitchen door and made a run for the bus.

"Lori, I'll come to the jail and talk to you later. Is there anyone you want me to call?"

"I guess I need a lawyer. And maybe you could let Nick know," she murmured, as the sheriff took her by the arm and led her out the door. The odd couple made their uncertain way across the lawn through a last scattering of children to the waiting police car.

XXVII

An interview in the rain

While Tasha Mulholland picked up hoops, shuttle cocks and racquets and stacked them in the shed that was the education center, she worried about Lori. It was obvious to everyone, especially Sheriff Stuart Mulholland, that the girl was guilty, but Tasha wasn't as certain—not for any good reason, but just because she couldn't believe Lori was a murderer. She and Adrian folded chairs and tables and took turns handing them up into the shed attic as the wind picked up and a storm began to grow in the sky. They tamed the tents that began rising up, billowing blue and white sails in a sea of grass, their pipes and chains rattling. "I don't believe she did it, Adrian," Tasha Mulholland shouted. They had done this together so many times, they knew each move, like dancers in something choreographed years before.

"You and the boys made the trap and she took the bait," he called back to her, the nasal whine of his voice almost animal in the singing wind. Together, they folded the last striped tent, and headed for the animal pen to clean up feathers and dung before everything got wet and mucky and smelled even worse. "I agree she's not what I would imagine a murderer to be, but she did conspire with me to make Aggie believe she was her daughter. She's not as innocent and helpless as she seems. She may be as conniving as I am."

"Why is she so passionate about being Aggie's daughter—it's as if she's not pretending at all. It's as if she really believes she is."

"What can I say? She persuaded herself. Like a new convert to a faith: God is my father; Aggie is my mother. Same idea."

"You helped it along, didn't you, you old cynic?"

"Yes, I suppose I did. And for a while, everyone was happy. She had a mother; Aggie had a daughter."

"And you were the father?"

"Yeah," he blushed and, not as watchful as he should have been, stepped in a sheep pile. "Oh, hell."

"How did it happen?" She grabbed a pail of sheep's drinking water at the side of the tent, and brought it over to him.

"Dunno. I just stepped in it."

"I don't mean that. How did you, an aspiring young museum curator, end up sleeping with a wealthy eccentric twenty years your senior and, I would guess, many years more experienced?"

He scraped at the sole of his shoe with a stick left over from a candied apple, then poured some of the water across it. Tasha found herself staring at the shoe, remembering the print Stuart had found. Size nine, cheaply made, the same configuration. "I tried to win her over, you know, for the sake of the museum. She loved beautiful young men. Unfortunately, I was just young and not at all beautiful, so we were only together the one time."

"And you didn't make her pregnant."

"No, but someone did. The accident happened later in the same year. Afterwards, she didn't remember who she had bedded when."

"You don't wear those shoes very often, do you Adrian?" Ms. Mulholland watched as he stood up and raked his foot through a patch of clean grass.

"Often enough," he said and looked at her sharply.

They finished cleaning up after the sheep as the dark flying clouds opened up and sheets of water spread out like curtains, cutting them off from the world around them with no one to see them, no cars or school buses splashing down the road, no one in sight anywhere. They sat together between the shed's open double doors, watching the rain. She didn't know what he was thinking, but she knew now that he had been in the root cellar at the museum the morning Aggie died and that she had no choice but to say something about it.

"You were there, weren't you, Adrian? You were with Aggie in the root cellar that morning."

He looked surprised. "Why would you think that? You don't think I did it, do you?" Lightning blanched his face to a white mask.

"I don't know what to think, but there was a bloody footprint in the root cellar, and the sole of your shoe is a perfect match for it." Thunder followed the lightning, rumbling across the sky. His face was deep in shadows now and she couldn't make it out.

"I was there," he said finally. "I found her dead in the root cellar. I didn't kill her. I didn't want Aggie dead. If anything, her death ended my chances of persuading her to leave something to the museum. I knew Lori had been there before me—I'd seen her coming out of the kitchen door, in fact, running. I was afraid she'd done it. In fact, it seemed obvious that she had. But what was I to do? I could have shut the door and left Aggie there. It might have been months before she was found, but that wouldn't have done me, or the Old Shrubsbury School House Museum any good. I didn't want her found in the root cellar. I didn't want anyone to know about the root cellar because I knew that Aggie was there for a reason and that the reason probably had to do with proving the existence of an heir besides Sera. But if I put the body somewhere—I thought the churn was inspired—and let it be discovered, maybe by you and me—I knew, you see, that she was making you her executrix—then I might have a second shot at proving Lori was Aggie's daughter. Or I might come up with some other scheme. Why not?"

"So that's why you're so sure Lori did it? You saw her. Did you confront her?"

"Oh, yes. And she agreed once again to share her inheritance with me, should she be the heir. She was scared. But Aggie had pretty much cut her out of the running, so there was no way Lori would ever be able to pay me for my silence. I didn't say anything because I didn't know how it would help my cause to do so. And the Howe connection? I tried to subvert it because I'd talked to Sera and she agreed to give me part of the money for the museum if I succeeded."

"I don't think Lori did it," Tasha said quietly.

"Then who? Because it wasn't me. Are you going to run to your son with this? I know it looks bad." He was silent, staring down at his twitching hands. "By the way, there was someone else there that morning, but I only saw them fleetingly."

"But you never thought the murderer might be that person instead of Lori?"

"Not really. Lori was such an obvious candidate. The other person wasn't."

"Was it a man or a woman? Where were they?"

"I'm not going to tell you, Tasha. At least not yet. So, are you going to tell your son about our conversation?"

"No. Or, as you say, not yet. Maybe, after I talk to Lori. But I don't think you did it, Adrian. You're not a murderer, even though you are ruthless. Incredibly ruthless."

"Thank you," Adrian said with a sheepish grin on his face. They sat and watched the rain until the curtain of water thinned to a scrim, and finally to mist.

As they swept the floors and locked up the shed, she asked him one last question: "Could Nick be Aggie's son? Is he a blood heir?"

"Oh, no. Not a chance. There's lots of evidence that he was

born well before the affair began. I think he's just a pretty boy who looks and acts a lot like his dad. Aggie wanted him to be the heir because she had a thing for his father, and then for him."

Tasha Mulholland took a shower before she went to the county jail to see Lori. She felt sullied by Adrian; she'd felt that way many times after conversations with him, even when murder and his indifference to other human beings weren't the subjects. She couldn't say why she continued to like him. Perhaps it was his passion for the past that was embodied in the museum. He reminded her of herself sometimes.

XXVIII

Lori

Lori sat at a small table in a gray featureless room across from Tasha Mulholland, her eyes swollen and red but dry at last, her lower lip quivering. "I didn't kill her."

"Why were you there, Lori? The meeting wasn't to be for a few hours."

"Is Nick coming?"

"I don't think so. He said you'd just have to bear up, wouldn't you, if you did it."

"So he thinks I did it. There's no trust between us, Tasha. I've thought many times that he might have murdered her."

"Listen, Lori. I've talked to Adrian and I know you were there very early. Why, if it wasn't to kill her?"

"I knew she would be there before dawn. She told me so, and I wanted to talk with her about us. I wanted to tell her I didn't want her money, I just wanted her friendship."

"Aggie is an odd mother figure. I'm afraid I can't understand why you were so intent on making her yours. She wasn't a nice person. You must have noticed that even when you were in her good graces."

"I don't know how to explain it."

"I think what I'm asking is whether you, more than you care to admit, wanted the financial security that being her daughter would bring?"

"She did owe me that. I tried so hard to be her daughter, the one Sera refused to be. I thought she'd be glad that Nick and I were dating. She'd loved his dad; she adored him. Maybe she'd welcome him as her heir. Then she told us she didn't want us together. Ever. As bizarre as it sounds, I think she wanted Nick for herself. And he wanted her money which, I think, is why he started taking me out—like me, he thought she'd like it. But when she didn't, we had to sneak around. She owed me something. I was a perfect daughter to her. I earned it."

"Oh, Lori. You don't earn a mother, especially a mother like Aggie." Tasha looked at her sadly. "Tell me, what happened that morning?"

"It was about 6:00 in the morning when I got to the museum. I'd run over in the early light; it takes me about twenty minutes from home. I remember the fog was so wet and heavy it was hard to breathe. The first thing that was odd was that the door was unlocked. Aggie usually locked it behind her. I looked for her first in the closet where I thought I might find her going over her notes, but she wasn't there.

"I called out her name and no one answered. That the closet

light was on made it even more eerie. I thought maybe she'd gone back home to get something and forgotten to lock the door. Then, just as I decided to go and see if she was at home, I swung my light around the kitchen. That's when I noticed the root cellar door was open. I don't think I'd ever seen it open before. I walked over and looked in and saw her there, all crumpled up on the floor. I'm afraid I don't remember much else. I don't think I stepped into the cellar—it was obvious she was dead. Her eyes were wide open." Lori shivered.

"I was standing there in the doorway next to the butter paddles. That's when I might have left something, though I can't imagine what. I was afraid the murderer was still there. I went out the kitchen door and ran. I never even locked it, I just ran. I ran for hours until it was time for the meeting. I didn't kill her, Ms. Mulholland, but I knew it would look as if I had. I'd been so vocal about my feelings about her. I'd probably even threatened her, I don't remember."

"Didn't you wonder why the door to the root cellar was closed and locked again when you came back?"

"Of course. Later Adrian told me he'd been there, but when I came back I had no idea Adrian had put her in the butter churn. I thought she was still in the root cellar. I asked about the churn because I was trying to change the subject. Everyone kept talking about where she might be."

"Can you remember anything odd when you first came into the building looking for her, anything at all? Close your eyes and try to recall from the moment you entered the museum."

Lori closed her eyes and rocked back and forth. "It was very quiet, I'd never heard it so quiet. My footsteps seemed so loud. But you're right, it did feel as if someone was there. I thought it was Aggie, of course. But she was already dead and this was like someone alive. Maybe it was the murderer."

"Where did you think he, or whoever it was, might be? In the next room? On the stairs? In the music room?"

"I don't know. I really don't. Does it matter?"

"Are you sure there was no one with Aggie in the root cellar?"

"No. I suppose there could have been someone crouched down in a corner or something. I saw the body and that was all I looked at." Her eyes were closed, remembering again. When she opened them she smiled, as if what she said next would make Ms. Mulholland feel better. "Adrian said he saw someone," she said hopefully.

Tasha Mulholland wasn't sure why, but she didn't want to talk about what she'd heard from Adrian or Lori to her son, the sheriff. She felt guilty about it, but she didn't want Adrian to go to jail; it was enough that Lori was there. She was sure they were both innocent. Still, it was obvious that Adrian could have been in the museum the whole time. He could have killed Aggie and then, hearing Lori come in, waited for her to leave. Why was it that she couldn't imagine him murdering anyone? Was she a detective with no understanding of people and no imagination besides? She looked forward to Alex coming the next day. A fresh perspective—a kid's perspective—might help.

But when Alex spread out on the living room floor with Winky the day after, she realized he wasn't going to be of any assistance at all. The boy was puffed up with his own testosterone. He'd had the best day of his young life at school. He and Coker told the story of Lori's entrapment and arrest over and over again. They were clever sleuths and everyone at Shrubsbury Elementary School knew it. Even the seventh and eighth graders were impressed with their prowess. With his milk glass raised, Alex proposed a toast: to the team of Churchill and Mulholland. He hadn't the slightest doubt that Lori did it. She'd always been odd and emotional and why not? He was fascinated by Adrian's story. Well, maybe Adrian then, maybe he did it. He was even odder. If they'd both been there that morning, if the bloody footprint belonged to Adrian, then it was even more likely that Adrian was the murderer. Two suspects. Now might be the time for a jury to move in and take over. They could decide. He and Ms. Mulholland had done all the hard work. So much for a kid's perspective.

Even though a seventh grader who had just won the admiration of his classmates was hard to talk to sensibly, she tried. "Why would Adrian have done it? He wouldn't have killed Aggie. He had no reason to."

"Maybe he'd just had it with her. I had."

"A long time ago, Alex, a very long time ago, he'd learned to live with her. And, by the way, you may have had it with her but you didn't kill her."

"Ms. M, I don't get it. Who do you think did it if Adrian or Lori didn't?"

"I don't know. Something is wrong. I just don't know what," she fretted.

Alex tried to give some credence to what she said. If she thought something was wrong, maybe it was. They were in the middle of a Chinese checkers game when he wondered aloud about the Sheltons' eBay site. "The bidding should have been over yesterday."

"Hmmmmm," responded Ms. Mulholland as she jumped one of his marbles. "That's something we, or at least I, forgot to look at closely. How did Adrian find that watercolor and acquire it so quickly the day after it was stolen? I got so caught up in the mystery of the painting itself that I forgot to push him on that. Did the Major call him? Or were he and the Major working together from the beginning? It had to be one or the other."

Distracted, Alex moved a marble into a vulnerable place and stared at her: "Ms. M, you're right. There's something fishy going on!"

She laughed as she took that marble and two more: "I think we need to know more about the Sheltons than we do."

XXIX

Alex goes visiting again

That evening Alex employed all his computer savvy to find out something, anything, about Major Shelton and Abigail Shelton. The sale had ended; the painting was sold. It looked as if the Major had also sold his melodeons, his chairs and his other paintings, and that he was pretty much through selling stuff. Alex found Abigail Shelton on Amazon where *Antiquities in New England* and *Vermont and Vermont Painters* were both listed. She was a scholar and probably smarter in important ways than the Major. Why oh why did she let him push her around the way he did? Why was she with him at all?

The Major was harder to investigate than his wife. Alex didn't have permission from Ms. M but he had her credit card number from their application to Ancestors.com, so he boldly logged onto Lost Persons.com and put charges on the card to get a closer look at Shelton. (He'd pay Ms. M back. He earned a weekly allowance; he was saving money for a new computer and already had thirty dollars.) As it turned out, Lemuel Shelton was only one name for a man who had a criminal record in New York State (embezzlement) and Connecticut (robbery).

Adrian had called an emergency board meeting for the next morning in the tea room across from the Old Shrubsbury School House Museum. If the Major went, and he almost always attended board meetings, his wife would be alone for a few hours. While Ms. Mulholland sat in the meeting and kept an eye on the Major and the rest of them, he'd pay Abigail Shelton a visit. He wanted to warn her and rescue her from the criminal Major. It would be the first time in his life he'd ever played hooky.

The next day, after his mother left for work, Alex mounted his bicycle and took off for the Shelton house. It was a morning full of crows cawing, a bright fall day, and the trees were redder than the last time he'd come this way. On the alert for cars heading his direction, every time he heard a motor he ditched his bike and hid until the vehicle passed. He was at the bottom of the Sheltons' hill when the Major came careening down the winding road, and he watched with satisfaction as the big purple car passed him on its way to the museum.

He'd never imagined Mrs. Shelton outside her house and by herself—she seemed so fragile—but Abigail Shelton was sitting in a white Adirondack chair on the crisply trimmed grass at the front of the house, drinking tea. It couldn't be coffee, there was something too airy about her for coffee. Her dress was a pale pink with big pockets like clusters of raspberries. She either looked very fashionable or very old-fashioned, he couldn't tell which.

She certainly didn't look like the other grown-ups he knew. She was staring into space, daydreaming, he guessed. It wasn't until he jumped off his bicycle that she saw him.

"Alex. Hello. What are you doing here?"

"Just out for a ride, Mrs. Shelton. I'm still doing body building."

"Oh, that's right. You're working on becoming an athletic brain, aren't you?"

"Yes, ma'am."

"Did you want to rest a minute? Can I get you something to drink?"

"No. I have water with me," he smiled and opened his blue plastic bottle and chug-a-lugged from it. He walked over and sat down on the lawn beside her.

"There's another chair over there next to the house."

"No, thank you." He figured he'd be more disarming if he acted like a kid and sprawled next to her on the lawn, and besides he could be closer to her and really study her face when he told her about her husband.

"I hear there's been a lot of excitement at the museum."

"Yes, ma'am," he answered, pleased that she'd given him an opening. "They caught Old Aggie's killer."

She smiled. "I've never heard Mrs. Hamilton called that." The grass was cool and comfortable. He liked being with her. She was the only beautiful woman he'd ever met.

"Yeah. Ms. Mulholland doesn't want me to call her that, but

I forget all the time."

"Well, I'm glad they found out who did it. You know Miss Chickering pretty well, don't you? She always seemed like such a nice person."

"She is. I didn't think she'd ever do anything like that."

"A lot of people aren't who they seem to be." He wondered if she was talking about her own experience, and he examined her face closely. Maybe she was beginning to realize how awful the Major was.

"I think Old Aggie hurt her feelings bad, and she couldn't get over it."

"Mrs. Hamilton was like that, wasn't she? Someone who hurt other people?"

"Yes." He turned over on his stomach, propped his chin in his hands, and looked up at her. "Lori told me she wanted Mrs. Hamilton to be her mother because her parents, who'd adopted her, hadn't been very nice."

"It doesn't seem like Agatha Hamilton was a very good choice to replace them, does it?"

"No, ma'am. Do you have nice parents?"

"They're okay, I guess. I was adopted too."

"When I met you the first time, I thought you must be the Major's daughter."

She laughed the way she always did, as if she had to be careful or the laugh would break apart and become something else. "Yes, people make that mistake. The Major is quite a lot older than I am. I was born in the mid '80s and he was born way back in the 1950s. I like to tease him about it."

"Where did you grow up, Mrs. Shelton?"

"Connecticut mostly."

"I guess lots of people did. Miss Chickering did. My principal did. Mrs. Hamilton was from there too."

"I'd heard that about Mrs. Hamilton."

"Did you like her?"

"I think I might have if she had let me. But she didn't like me. Not even a little."

"Yeah. She didn't think much of me either."

They laughed together. The silence afterwards was uncomfortable. "I don't think Miss Chickering did it," he said abruptly.

"Oh, my. I thought she had confessed."

"No. She says she was there but Aggie had already been killed."

"Heavens. Does she have any idea who did it?"

"I don't know. Mr. Dabney was there too."

"You mean he may have done it?"

"I suppose maybe, but Ms. Mulholland doesn't think so and he says not. But he was there and saw someone besides Miss Chickering."

She looked down at him. He couldn't tell what her expression meant, whether she was alarmed or not. She seemed to be on the edge of something he'd never seen on her face before. "Alex, why did you ride up here this morning?"

"I told you. Just exercise."

"I don't believe you." She looked down at him intently and put her hand in her pocket. He moved to a sitting position. If she had a gun in her pocket—or a bread knife—he was ready to make a run for it. "I don't know anything about Mrs. Hamilton's murder. Did you think I might?"

"I thought the Major might and since you're his wife, you might too."

"He doesn't, I don't. I don't know who you think we are, but we're just people on the periphery. Except for selling paintings to some of the odd sorts around here, we don't have anything to do with the drama around Mrs. Hamilton."

He'd have to ask Ms. Mulholland the meaning of periphery sometime. Whatever it meant, he was sure it didn't apply to the Sheltons. "You stole the watercolor by Nate Howe."

She didn't respond.

"And then Mr. Dabney got it from you. You're in this with him, aren't you?" He was on his feet now. He might have to move fast.

She sat up straight in her chair. "Get out of here, Alex. Quickly. Go!" He didn't need to hear her say it again. Her face was dark with fear, but he could see anger too. She was trembling and he wondered if she was going to have a fit.

He got on his bike and rode out fast.

About halfway down the hill, he realized why she'd put her hand in her pocket. She wasn't fumbling for a gun or a knife. She was looking for her cell phone to call her husband.

Alex figured he'd better get to the museum before Major Shelton had time to think through his next move, before Adrian was in trouble and before Ms. Mulholland was in even bigger trouble. The Major might want to kill Adrian if he believed he could identify him as the murderer. Or probable murderer. He might want to do in Ms. M just because she knew things—way too many things. Like an Olympian, he jumped his bike over ditches and rocks, still listening for cars, diving into the bush when a jeep passed, when a truck rattled by, when the big purple car roared toward him. Alex watched from behind a tree as it passed, then ditched his bicycle in a grove of trees and took a shortcut on foot.

He called on his experience as a scout and a hiker. He knew that where there were creeks and where there was running water, the way would be clearer. There might be some water in the summer-dry beds, but there would be less scrub. He knew where he had to jump fences, where there was a scary bull in one field and a wrathful farmer in another, and where he had to cross public roads. There were newly cut hay fields he could run through, but he had to be careful or he'd be visible from the road. He cut through two cornfields, careful to consult his compass because it was easy to lose all sense of direction in the middle of tall corn. He went through two small woods, but the road was close by. The Major roared by once, twice, even three times. He never caught sight of Alex.

XXX

A meeting of the board

So far the emergency meeting hadn't been very helpful. Winifred Persinger, the president, was leading the group in an anxious conversation to decide how they could deflect publicity about the murder and now the capture of the murderer, the museum's very own assistant director, on Fall Harvest Day. Ms. Mulholland's presence was mandatory since she could help ensure that the boundaries of the museum were as closed to the press as possible.

"I wish Lori would confess so it could all be put behind us quickly. What do you think the chances of that are, Adrian?" asked Winifred Persinger.

"Poor, I'm afraid." Adrian pushed back his chair and looked moodily out the window.

"So there could be a long trial?"

"I'm afraid so. We're going to have to think long term. She already has a defense attorney and he plans to prove that there are other parties just as likely to have done it."

"Oh, my. Who?"

"So far? Aggie's daughter, Sera. Principal Plumbwell. Me."

"Principal Plumbwell? Why you, of all people?" asked the local librarian.

"Agatha Hamilton and I had some rather public disputes."

"You and everyone else," said George Sampson, the plump banking heir and museum treasurer. "But you're a school principal, for God's sake."

"Does that mean, George, that you think a museum director is a more likely murderer than a school principal?" asked Mrs. Persinger.

There was merriment around the big oak table, but no one thought it all that amusing. Not really. Several people refilled their coffee cups. George Sampson, who'd been trying to lose weight and had resisted picking up any of the powdered doughnut holes the local librarian bought at the Quick Stop, finally gave into temptation and took two.

It was then that Major Shelton received a phone call. Excusing himself, he headed for the hallway. After rumbling for minutes in a voice too low for anyone to make out words, he returned and excused himself again, claiming a family emergency, nothing serious, his wife had locked herself out and everyone knew how emotional she could be. He'd come back if he could. Please continue the meeting without him.

Tasha Mulholland and Adrian Dabney looked after him anxiously. No one else paid much attention.

The board members all agreed to lower the profile of the museum temporarily. They concluded that it should be shut down immediately, almost a month before its usual closing date. The crafts classes could continue, but the advertising for them would be limited to ads in the classified. Any efforts by the media to interview staff or board members would be discouraged. No one would be permitted to take pictures inside the museum, and while they couldn't keep people from photographing its exterior, they would discourage parking and picture taking by putting "No Parking" signs everywhere. With Sera Hamilton's permission—was she the right person to ask?—they would extend the "No Parking" perimeter to the Hamilton House.

Finally, they decided, they'd leave everything in the capable hands of their director, Adrian Dabney. The press would talk only to him. Everyone else would keep mum. Ms. Mulholland looked across the table at him and shook her head almost sternly. "I think," she said, "that Adrian's role in this drama may make that difficult."

Adrian sighed, wishing she weren't here. "She's right," he said. "My relationships with the deceased and the accused are too complicated. We'd do better to make Mrs. Persinger our spokesperson."

"So, Winifred, are you willing to assume responsibility for press relations, at least until this thing blows over?" asked Harold Plumbwell.

"Yes. Yes, I am. Someone has to do it. You can refer all the phone calls and e-mails to me, and I'll do my best to keep it all under control. But there must be someone on site also. And since Adrian's not able to take on that task, I nominate you, Tasha."

"I'll do my best. Except for the occasional crafts class, we'll keep the museum zipped up."

There was general assent around the table, people nodding and uh huhhing, so glad that the responsibility had been passed on to others, so glad that they could go home soon, proud that they'd made decisions, and relieved that they didn't have to make more, at least not about this. They went on to committee reports: the treasurer, events, the gift shop, the grounds, the education program and its very successful, until Lori's surrender, birthday event for the Rev. Evensong and Fall Harvest Day, acquisitions....

Ms. Mulholland was listening without much enthusiasm to a report about a bequest of tea china to the museum when she caught sight of Alex at the window, bouncing up and down frantically. "Excuse me," she murmured, rising. "I'm going to have to leave early. There's something I must attend to."

Outside, Alex was waiting for her eagerly. His clothes were covered with burrs, and his face was streaked with dirt. Ms. Mulholland took him to the back of the building to sit on the stone bench that looked out over the farm pond. "Why aren't you in school? What happened?"

She listened carefully to his story, and wondered how much of his excitement was what small boys experience when they play cowboys and Indians, or today—more likely—Star Trek, and how much was rooted in reality. "Why did you do that, Alex? Why did you let her know we suspect her husband of killing Mrs. Hamilton, especially after you found out he has a criminal record?"

"I don't know. I like her. I wanted to warn her so she could get away from him before we move in on him. But I think someone had better help protect Mr. Dabney, especially if he really did see Major Shelton."

Tasha Mulholland sent Alex in to clean himself up as well as he could, then called her son and left a message. A sheriff should be easier to find, she muttered to herself. She and Alex were crossing the road to make certain the museum was closed up tight when the Major drove up.

The big man rolled down the window of his car and boomed at her: "Your blithering idiot of a boy has frightened my poor Abigail to death. I want him kept away from us; I'll get a restraining order if necessary."

"Major Shelton, please. I think you must be exaggerating. How can a boy's twaddle have upset her so badly?"

"He practically accused me of murdering the old lady, that's how. Most people might be able to fend off that kind of creepy fantasizing. My wife is very sensitive and frightened of the least thing. She's been very kind to him. I don't know why he wants to persecute her. Keep him away from respectable people, or his mother will be the next to hear from me."

"Major, it's true that Alex is an imaginative boy, but I don't think that he meant to outright accuse you of murder, however suggestive your criminal record might be."

The Major looked at her and reddened. "Madame, I assure you, I've paid for every mistake I've made in my life. If you want to accuse me of something, please do it publicly. Don't send a nasty scamp to my house to terrify my wife." He paused to catch his breath before he continued: "I've got something else to settle with you, Ms. Mulholland, some information I don't think you're yet aware of. I talked with Rupert Young this morning. I think I may be able to solve your problems with regard to Mrs. Hamilton's will."

"And how will you do that, Major?"

"Call Young. He'll tell you how." He gunned his motor and his wheels screeched as he drove off to park his car. Ms. Mulholland and Alex watched him squeeze free from the big car like an enraged bull caught in a space too small, and charge up the path back to the meeting.

Ms. Mulholland gazed after him for a few moments, then continued to the museum. Gravely, she handed the big skeleton key to Alex so he could lock the door. Then she turned to him and smiled. "I've baked some ginger snaps. We can eat and talk. We may be almost ready to close this case."

XXXI

Who inherits? Who goes to prison?

Tasha Mulholland had asked everyone to come to the kitchen of the Old Shrubsbury School House Museum at 9:00 in the morning. There was poetic justice, she thought, in bringing them back together at the same time of day as the original meeting. For Alex's sake, she didn't invite his mother. She hoped Donna Churchill would never know how involved her son had been in murder. Three people had been added to the company: Rupert Young, Esq.; Sheriff Stuart Mulholland and Sera Hamilton. Ms. M and Alex had collected chairs and brought them down to the kitchen where they'd set them in a ragged but intimate circle.

It was another of those fall days when the wind blew and sunlight danced in the kitchen, when one hundred and fifty and more years ago a bunch of students sat around the fire, peeling and cutting up apples to cook for sauce, telling each other stories, and comparing notes on what seemed to a twenty-first century kid the weirdest but most curious of subjects: the meaning of Plato's shadow wall in the contemporary world, the nature of reality and the end of the world. Ms. M and Alex would talk about it all soon, when he was a little older.

"It feels like she's here, doesn't it?" said Alex.

"You mean Aggie?"

"Yeah."

They sat and waited, neither saying much, both of them nervous.

Sera was the first to arrive. She took a seat by the fireplace where the stone formed a perfect backdrop for her mass of red hair and another frock of the same not-quite-shocking-shade-of-purple. Staring at Tasha Mulholland hard and long, as if she hoped to intimidate her into turning over every cent and square foot of her mother's estate, she seemed focused and sharp as a knife, though perhaps not a bread knife—something longer, leaner, and more effective. She couldn't have killed her mother, Ms. Mulholland thought. It was hard to picture Sera with a bread knife at all. If she were going to kill, the weapon would be more important. And there'd be an audience.

They talked nervously about the weather.

The next to arrive were Major and Mrs. Shelton. When he introduced Sera to his wife, the big woman stared at her just as she had Ms. Mulholland, but with even more intensity. Abigail Shelton paled and shrank back into herself. "You look familiar," said Sera. "Surely, we've met somewhere before." Tasha Mulholland found it almost amusing that both women had the same deep-set nearly purple eyes.

Harold Plumbwell arrived with all his resentments sprouting like poisonous weeds around him. "I can't stay long, Ms. Mulholland. I hope this will be short." He shut his mouth and glared when Sheriff Stuart Mulholland followed him into the room with Lori in tow. A lawman might not be as easily bullied. A subdued Lori stared down at the floor, and followed the sheriff's instructions to take a seat. She squirmed uneasily when Nick Crafts appeared. "Hi, Tasha everyone. Isn't it a beautiful day? Nothing like autumn in Vermont. Have you finally figured out how to dispose of Mrs. Hamilton's estate?"

He was so cheerful. So charming, Ms. Mulholland had to smile. She didn't answer him because she was interrupted by Adrian's grand entrance with the lawyer Rupert Young, Esq. Ms. M rose to greet the attorney, shaking his hand, murmuring pleasantries. He and Adrian took the last remaining chairs.

No one seemed to have anything to say to anyone else, so Tasha started the meeting without any of the usual formalities. "Thank you for coming to the kitchen again," she said and looked from person-to-person pleasantly. "There are two reasons for this meeting: to establish Agatha Hamilton's heir, and her killer. The two subjects are closely related, which has placed me in the unfamiliar role of detective. Alex has been my close associate in this adventure. He and I have been studying Aggie's murder for some time now, figuring that an old woman and a twelve-year old boy would fall under everyone's radar, especially the killer's. It's been hard because the murder was so gruesome and neither of us was happy to imagine any of you as the killer. Nonetheless, we're convinced one of you is."

"I hope you won't beat around the bush, Ms. Mulholland. This isn't an Agatha Christie novel," snapped Rupert Young. Sera and Adrian laughed; apparently no one else read mysteries that old-fashioned.

"I'll try to keep it brief, Rupert. But I think it's important that you understand what's happened here since some legal decisions may need to be made even after Aggie's heir has been determined.

"As most of you probably know by now, Rupert Young informed me after Agatha Hamilton's death that she had made me her executrix. She'd never asked me and I wasn't happy about the task, which was to decide who was entitled to her fortune and her house—but I've done my best to serve her interests.

"The obvious heir was Serendipity Hamilton, but Sera and Agatha Hamilton never got along, and Aggie threatened many times to disinherit her. There can be no doubt that she was a terrible mother. Even the name she gave you at birth was ambiguous," she said, looking sympathetically at Sera. "Serendipity. Your birth was a random event. An accident. In her notes to Mr. Young and myself, she asked that I ignore you unless I drew a blank on all the other possibilities. I had a month to pursue them."

Sera Hamilton nodded grimly.

"Aggie had another child about thirty years ago, in 1972, but the birth occurred shortly after she was incapacitated by an accident. Her husband, who may or may not have been the child's father, gave the baby away while Aggie was comatose, and when she revived she was happy for his decision. He died soon after, and no record seems to have been left about where the child went. Lori, with the connivance of Adrian, tried to convince Aggie that she was that child. Lori was to give Adrian a sizeable chunk of Aggie's money, plus the house, in return. Adrian has been open about his scam. It was all for the museum, of course, which is the great love of his life."

Adrian smiled sheepishly. "I confess it. What should have mattered to Aggie was this place. It nurtured her and her ancestors. But she disowned it."

"If Aggie had been killed when the scam was discovered, you or Lori would have been the obvious suspects. But Aggie guessed you were scamming her months ago. As it is, neither of you seems to have had much of a motive for murder. Although, Lori's disappointment and rage when Agatha Hamilton rejected her might have been sufficient."

"I didn't do it, Ms. Mulholland. I really didn't."

"I know, Lori. I know you didn't."

"She was just in the wrong place at the wrong time," Alex added, to no one in particular.

"None of us knew that Aggie had been told by her doctor that she probably had only a short time left," Tasha Mulholland continued. "It might have saved her life if the killer had known. She was determined to make plans. She hated you so much, Adrian,

239

that she had no intention of leaving anything to the museum. She cared enough about family lineage so that she continued to look for relations.

"Aggie had always assumed that her ancestor, Audrey West, had been the only one of two female children of the original owner of the Hamilton House, to bear children. The other sister, Juliette Whittington, and her husband had been painted by Nathan Howe, a well-known primitive painter of the day, and their portraits were upstairs here at the museum. Aggie's hopes for a distant cousin to give her money to were raised when a baby began to emerge in Juliette's portrait, a baby who had been painted out probably not long after the painting was made, and who reappeared after one hundred and sixty-five years, when the paint that covered her began to fade away. The explanation that seemed to make the most sense was that the baby had died. But there was no proof of that, just as there was no actual proof that she'd ever existed. There had always been rumors and stories. Aggie had long ago discounted them. There was a genealogy made twenty-five years ago that suggested Juliette had had a baby, but none of the other genealogies made over the years showed one. Aggie surrendered to their judgment, until she saw that image. She was the first to see it, and the only one for months. No one else noticed. It was about the same time that Harold Plumbwell came to Shrubsbury. Although Harold is known to all of us as the principal of our local school, and even though he has a bachelor's degree in nineteenth century history, he's also a confidence man who's wanted in Connecticut, which is where Aggie met him years ago."

"You just stepped over the line, old lady. I can sue for defamation of character, and I will." Harold Plumbwell stood up menacingly. Stuart rose and advanced towards him. Plumbwell sat down again.

"When you and Aggie first met, you didn't like each other. You both moved on. More recently, while you were looking for a new scheme and reviewing the rich people you'd known over the years, you remembered Aggie. At the time you were reading about the painter Nathan Howe—in a book, incidentally, by Mrs. Shelton. You discovered that the painter's family tree included an illegitimate daughter in Vermont. Howe's own tree ended close enough to your own that you thought, with a few dodges and some made-up in-betweens, you might convince Aggie you were her cousin. You remembered her; you thought she might be crazy enough to buy the idea. You created a genealogy for yourself and brought it to Vermont. She never thought it was authentic but she let you think she was checking it out, and having discovered that you'd do anything for a dollar, she enlisted you in a search for real evidence of the baby's birth. She also made you her spy on the Old Shrubsbury School House board."

"I don't have to sit here and listen to this calumny," muttered Plumbwell.

"Plumbwell, you heard the lady," said Stuart. "I have a deputy outside who's prepared to hold you on a Connecticut arrest warrant. Behave yourself."

Alex almost laughed out loud. Wait until they heard about this at school.

"After Aggie's death, you were ready to resume your scam with the executrix, namely me. You planted a fake baptismal certificate you and Aggie designed for baby Isabelle at the site of Nate Howe's cellar hole. You'd convinced Nick to let me know about the site. You knew that Alex and I would be exploring it, so you placed the certificate in the wall where we were certain to look. I'm not sure how you thought you would eventually win out over Nick. I am sure he knew what you were about."

Alex watched the two men glare at each other. Nick was a total jerk. How could he have ever liked him?

"Not long before the baby's first appearance, the Sheltons came to town and informed Agatha Hamilton about Mrs. Shelton's books and her expertise on Howe. Aggie went to their website and saw the second Howe painting, a picture of a hill opposite her window. It had been painted in the same year as Juliette's portrait. Mrs. Hamilton knew the painting and the scene. Since it was outside her bedroom window, she'd looked at the scene most of her life. The painting itself had been her family's before it belonged to the museum, and before it was stolen. She knew that Nate Howe's house should have been where the sheep were—but wasn't, not as far as she could tell. Alex discovered that the house had been painted out with a flock of sheep and was re-emerging when he visited the Sheltons a couple of weeks ago."

"You should have told me what you were doing. We had no

idea why everyone wanted the painting," Mrs. Shelton murmured, looking very pretty, he thought, in a flowery dress patterned with flowers the color of her eyes.

Ms. Mulholland continued. "To Mrs. Hamilton, the Sheltons were clearly thieves. She had them investigated and confirmed it. She could have informed the proper authorities, but she was more interested in using the painting to make her case and made a high bid on it. She planned to turn the two of you in as soon as she'd acquired the painting. I don't know whether you realized that, Major Shelton?"

The Major looked uneasy, as if he might make a break for it, but remembering the deputies the sheriff said were outside, he decided he'd do better to wait and see what happened next.

"Baby Isabelle was apparently the illegitimate daughter of Nathan Howe and Juliette Whittington. Nate Howe, in painting out his own house, seemed to be trying to blot out his presence in the lives of Juliette and her daughter. At least, that was a possible interpretation. Mrs. Hamilton liked it. She knew that there was a Howe watercolor in the Shrubsbury town room that might be a third painting in Howe's narrative. It was painted at the same time as the two others, and it was of an odd and extremely unlikely subject for the time and the painter. That's why she was exploring the root cellar in the museum the day she was killed. She didn't know exactly what she was looking for; she hoped for proof of Isabelle's birth. Alex and I think she also guessed that the root cellar in question could be at Nate Howe's home site. At any event, she hoped evidence of Isabelle's birth was one place or the other. With or without that proof she was looking forward to telling everyone about the picture narrative and Juliette's child. It was a way of sticking it to Adrian and Lori. She also wanted to needle Mr. Plumbwell.

"Agatha Hamilton had been searching for a legitimate heir to replace Sera for some time. Then Nick Crafts came into her life, the son of the only man she'd ever really loved. I'm guessing here, Nick—you must have seemed very much like your father to her. As we all know, she wasn't well mentally. You took advantage of that. You let her think you cared. You played her fair-haired boy because you wanted her money and her house. She'd put Plumbwell to work constructing proof that you were the descendent of Isabelle, letting him believe for a while, at least, that he was still working on his own genealogy. She knew she couldn't prove anything since there was no truth in it, but she thought she could put together a good enough case to make it almost impossible for Sera to contest the will."

Nick blushed a deep red. "I made her happy. You're right that I did it for her money, but I did make her happy."

"Of course, none of that matters since Alex and his friend Coker dug up a death certificate for Isabelle. Nathan Howe's and Juliette Whittington's baby only lived for a few months. Mrs. Hamilton, had she lived and discovered that proof, would have had to create another scenario for Nick Crafts. And very well might have."

Alex looked properly somber: Ms. Mulholland expected it of him.

Tasha Mulholland looked over at him and smiled fondly. "Alex and I wondered why we were included in Mrs. Hamilton's invitation to the kitchen that morning. I discovered I'd been invited because she'd made me her executrix. Not long ago, we found out that Alex is Nate Howe's great-grandson three times removed from his relationship with his wife, not Juliette. Mrs. Hamilton didn't really like him; children never pleased her. But I think she saw him as one more way to aggravate everyone else, especially if she implied that he might get some money. I don't think she ever had any intention of actually giving him something.

"Finally, the Sheltons were invited because they had the second painting, even though they didn't really know what its significance was to Mrs. Hamilton. She looked forward to letting the world know about it, and how it had been stolen years before from the Old Shrubsbury School House. She planned to take care of the Sheltons that day too.

"So, you see, there were quite a few people here on the day Aggie was killed who had some reason to kill her."

The room was quiet except for the wind outside. Alex looked around at the people who had dominated his imagination for so many weeks. All of them were guilty, he thought. Not of the murder, but of deceit. They were all liars. He bet the kids who used to live here were better people than these. And the Rev. Evensong? He would have been so angry. That grim stocky fellow in the clerical collar would have called down the wrath of God on them all.

Ms. Mulholland took a sip of water and a deep breath. "Perhaps no one had more reason to kill than Major Shelton. For a long time Alex and I thought the Sheltons were just petty thieves. Since, we've learned at least some of what Aggie knew about their criminal past. And about Adrian's involvement. He knew about the picture narrative; Aggie told him something about it the day before her death. Afterwards, he visited the Sheltons and looked at the second painting. He was one of the people bidding on it. The other two were Harold Plumbwell and Nick Crafts. None of them was interested in it for aesthetic or historical reasons. Adrian didn't even care that it had been stolen from the museum years before. Nor did he want to trace any ancestor for Agatha Hamilton. On the contrary, he wanted to discredit any proof that there was an Isabelle who grew up and had children who had children. He knew that if either Nick or Harold won the inheritance, his hopes for money for the museum were over. But there were so many angles to play in Adrian's world."

She pivoted and looked at Adrian, sitting quietly, chin in hand, fascinated by the story Ms. M was telling. "You suggested to Sera that you and she could share Aggie's fortune if you could put an end to the search for another heir. Not long after you made the same kind of offer to Major Shelton and Abigail Shelton. You'd keep your mouth shut about everything if the museum got a considerable share of anything they inherited. You played every angle."

"But why did he think Major and Mrs. Shelton had any possibility of inheriting?" asked Nick.

"Because Adrian found out one more thing: Lemuel Shelton and Abigail Shelton aren't husband and wife. They're father and daughter. Or rather, stepfather and daughter. He deduced, I'm not sure how, perhaps they told him, that Abigail was the baby who was left in a Connecticut orphanage all those years ago, the child Aggie gave birth to but never met. The Sheltons were here to claim Abigail's rightful inheritance from Agatha Hamilton. I think they've told you about Abigail Shelton's claim, Mr. Young?"

"Indeed, they have. Just yesterday. And I should add that it's a persuasive one."

"I'm sure it is. They've been slow to bring it forward. When they first came, they made a disastrous impression on Aggie. She especially didn't like Abigail, despite the fact that the young woman had made herself an expert on Nathan Howe. The Major observed what happened to Sera; he knew they would have to be very careful with Aggie. Trying to mollify her wouldn't work. When he told her about her daughter that day in the root cellar, she told him she didn't care, that Nick was the rightful heir. So he killed her, figuring that they'd have a better legal chance at the money if Aggie was dead."

"What kind of a story is that? You don't have any proof," blustered the Major.

Ms. Mulholland ignored him. "When Lori was arrested, the Sheltons had it made. The murderer was found, they could relax and claim Abigail's inheritance. But someone else saw the murderer that day. Adrian didn't kill Aggie, but he did find her

247

body after Lori had discovered it. He saw Lori leaving, running, in fact, and he assumed that she had committed the murder. He put Mrs. Hamilton in the butter churn. He didn't want anyone finding out about the root cellar and chasing down clues about another heir. Adrian didn't know that he'd left a shoe print in the root cellar so that his own presence had been betrayed. He could be arrested on suspicion of murder. In fact, there's more to tie him to the murder than Lori. That's why I know Adrian will tell us who else he saw that morning and has been trying to blackmail. I imagine that person is Major Shelton."

Adrian looked at Ms. Mulholland quizzically. Then, shrugging his shoulders and smiling his odd smile, he told her: "You're wrong. I didn't see Major Shelton that morning."

"Then who, Adrian? Or am I wrong and you murdered her?"

"Oh, no. I didn't kill Aggie. Wouldn't have. Couldn't have. I almost loved her once. No, the person I saw was Mrs. Shelton. Abigail Shelton, Aggie's daughter."

Abigail Shelton stood up, and staggered towards him. The Major caught her, holding her back. "What a piece of work," she said. "You're something else, Adrian Dabney." She broke away, her eyes large, anger distorting the features Alex had found so lovely. "Yes, I killed her. We'd given her every proof of my birth; she had to know she was my mother. And she spat at me. I'm not speaking in metaphors. She spat at her own daughter."

Sera laughed hoarsely. Abigail turned and glared at her: "Hah! What kind of daughter were you, you overblown cartoon of a woman?" Sera rose up like some beast of prey provoked, and took two long strides towards the pale, wispy name-caller who claimed to have murdered her mother. She towered over her. No one knew what to expect, but before she could do anything, Abigail Shelton turned her back on her. Confused, Sera moved away from the woman who had turtled down now, crouching over her handbag, moaning.

"Abigail Shelton," intoned Sheriff Stuart Mulholland, sounding very lawman-like. "You're under arrest."

She rose, and whirled around to face everybody. There was something in her extended hand, a gun, a small pearl-handled gun, the perfect gun for her, thought Alex, and despite everything, he found himself admiring her stance and how, even now, she was movie star perfect.

Ms. Mulholland looked over at Stuart: "Do something!" she said. No one moved.

"Abigail Shelton," said Sheriff Stuart Mulholland again, his voice filling the room, "Put down the gun; raise your hands. You're in enough trouble already; you don't want to hurt anyone."

"Hey, Abby, don't fool around with that thing. We'll get you a good lawyer. Don't do this," said the Major.

"Sure we will. Why should I do anything you say? You're the guy who's been fooling around with those silly Howe paintings for the last month. A lot of help you've been."

"Come on, sweetheart. You don't want to shoot anyone."

"Like you? Maybe you're the one I should shoot." She waved

the gun in his direction; he cowered.

Uncertain what was behind her, slowly, almost clumsily, she backed toward the kitchen door, gun raised. Alex was sitting there, looking at her in bewilderment. Where was the sweet woman he thought he loved? She sensed he was there, and leaning sideways, grabbed his arm and pulled him to his feet and towards her.

"Alex is going to help me escape, aren't you? No one follow me; if you do I'll shoot the boy." She jammed the gun into his ribs. "Just stay where you are, all of you." She was out the door with a surprised Alex.

"She's heading for our car," the Major said in the flat voice of someone in shock. "She has keys."

Stuart Mulholland, his own gun drawn, followed at a safe distance. Ms. Mulholland stood at the kitchen door. She tried prayer, she tried coming up with a plan, she thought about running after them but the car was close by so they were already there.

That was when Alex got mad. He wasn't really angry at Abigail Shelton and there was no reason to be angry at anyone else. He was angry at a world where the kids at school would hear about the wimpy woman who held their schoolmate, Alex, hostage, and drove him to his doom in a car the color of an eggplant. He saw their pitying faces—poor, poor Alex—and heard their giggles when the grown-ups weren't listening. So much for his dreams of being smart and cool.

"Get in," she said, pointing the gun at him.

"No."

"For God's sake, Alex, get in. I don't want to hurt you."

"You won't hurt me because you need me. If you shoot me, you won't have a hostage any more and the sheriff will come running. You're stuck, you know. There's nothing you can really do except give up. Besides, you didn't exactly kill Aggie all by yourself. You have to stay around to make sure the Major gets his."

Abigail Shelton's grip on his arm loosened. "No. Of course not. You're right." She looked at the advancing sheriff. She looked around, as if there might be someone somewhere to help. "Even so, please Alex, please get into the car," she pleaded. "I don't want to shoot you. I just don't want to go to prison."

"If you run now, no one will know about the Major. No one will know about Mr. Dabney." He leaned against the car like the coolest guy ever. Abigail Shelton was crying, her gun hand was going limp. Sheriff Stuart Mulholland was closing in. She shrugged as Alex took the gun from her and handed it to Stuart.

XXXII

Accessory to murder

A lex wasn't as heroic when it was over. He couldn't stop shaking. Ms. Mulholland grabbed him the way his mother would have if she'd been there. There was no help for it. The older women in his life loved him and he had to let them have their way with him.

Stuart was reading Abigail Shelton her rights and at the same time handcuffing her.

The Major was trying to figure out how to get past them all to his big purple car; Principal Plumbwell was dashing for his black one. Fortunately, Stuart had brought deputies enough for everybody.

Tasha Mulholland invited the members of the gathering who were still present—Lori, Nick, Sera, Rupert Young, Esq., and Adrian Dabney—to join her and Alex for coffee, tea and more conversation in the meeting room across the road. No one wanted to go back to the kitchen.

They sat down around the big table in a state of confusion.

"That didn't go exactly as I had hoped," Ms. Mulholland said ruefully. She was making coffee in the corner as she spoke. It was the ordinary coffee they drank at board meetings—Alex knew she couldn't stand the stuff.

"Did you want some tea, Rupert?" she asked, using the lawyer's first name without thinking about it, just glancing in his direction.

"Yes, please Ms. Mulholland," he replied, not seeming to notice the intimacy. "I'm afraid you and I have further business, don't we? It doesn't look like Abigail Shelton will be available to inherit."

"Yo man, are you all right?" Nick asked Alex. Alex was still shaking.

"Yeah, just a little after shock, I guess."

"You're quite a kid. You have no idea how much I wanted to be like you were today when I was your age," Nick grinned. Alex stared down at his shoes. He could say something, but he didn't want his voice to turn all soprano and trembly the way it might if he told Nick what he thought of him. He looked over at Lori who hadn't stopped crying. Almost as if she thought she was still under arrest.

"No," Tasha Mulholland said to the lawyer. "I guess Abigail Shelton will be otherwise occupied. It's a shame."

"She deserves a medal of honor, not prison," said Sera Hamilton. "I didn't have the guts to take the old woman down. She did."

"I think Aggie's behavior towards her may stand her in good

stead with a jury," Tasha answered her with a broad grin.

"So now what, Ms. Mulholland?" the lawyer asked. "Our month is almost out."

"Neither of Mrs. Hamilton's plans for her fortune panned out. Her only relative besides Sera is on her way to prison. Juliette Whittington's baby died decades ago, and there is no long lost cousin. I'm sure she would have liked to hand everything over to Nick, but she was sure Sera would contest it, and so she tried to prove he was related. But you're not, are you Nick?"

"No. I'm afraid not," he smiled sadly. "I would have liked the money. I figured she kind of owed me. Her affair with my dad made my home life miserable as a kid, and especially when we had to move to get away from her."

"Mrs. Hamilton certainly didn't want to give her money to the Old Shrubsbury School House Museum," mused Ms. M. "So you've lost out, Adrian. I think Aggie's daughter, Sera, is the obvious person to inherit, Rupert. Don't you?"

"I do think most of the money will come to you in the end, Miss Hamilton. But the red tape may take time to unravel."

"Maybe I can convince Sera to share some of her mother's fortune with the museum," murmured Adrian.

Ms. Mulholland poured hot water in the prettiest cup she could find, dunked a tea bag in it, and took it over to Rupert Young. "Not quite up to Earl Grey, I'm afraid."

He looked up at her coldly. "It will do, thank you, Ms. Mulholland."

"After all," said Adrian, "she and her mother grew up in the shadow of the museum. She knows I tried to help her get her inheritance."

"You can speak directly to me, Adrian. I don't know how hard you tried, but I don't think you're the reason I may have won out."

"Oh, my darling. You don't know the half of what I've been through."

"Sorry, Adrian. As far as I'm concerned, our agreement is null and void."

Stuart Mulholland appeared at the door.

"Would you like some coffee, dear?" asked his mother.

"Yes, please." He sat down next to Alex. "How are you doing, young man?"

"Fine. I'm okay."

"You did great. What in the world were you and she talking about out there?"

Ms. Mulholland poured coffee all around, except to the tea-drinker Rupert Young, took the pot back to the stove, and sat down to listen to Alex and Stuart.

"I told her that she couldn't shoot me because if she did she'd lose me as a hostage and she'd be caught."

"Yeah, that was good. It confused her didn't it?"

"Yeah. Then I told her that if she ran away, the guy who helped her do the murder would get away scot free. That confused her even more."

"My God, this coffee is bad," murmured Ms. M. Alex grinned.

"I guess. Do you think she knew the Major was making a run for it?" asked Nick.

"I think she expected that and I don't think she cared much. He was always mean to her. But the Major wasn't who I was talking about."

"Yeah, I didn't think so," said Stuart.

"Yeah, Ms. M and I figured it out yesterday when we were planning this meeting. We thought everybody would see it right away."

"Oh, my Lord. More Christie," muttered Rupert Young. "Ms. Mulholland, I beg you, let us all in on your little secret so we can get back to the real business of this world."

"The getting and disposing of money," breathed Sera.

"Think," said Tasha Mulholland, looking proudly at her son and her surrogate grandson. "Abigail Shelton was far too small and delicate a woman to have opened the root cellar door for Aggie. Even together the two women couldn't have done it. Remember what an effort it was for the police to open it later that day."

"My God, of course," says Nick Crafts. "Lori might have been able to get it open, but not Mrs. Shelton. So who opened it?"

"The same man who later, after hiding Aggie's body in the butter churn, closed it again."

Everyone looked expectantly at Adrian, who shrugged. "Yes, I opened it for Aggie. That doesn't mean that I helped murder her."

"We're not sure you didn't egg poor Abigail on. You were there the whole time, Adrian. You were there to open the door;

you were there with Abigail; you were there with Lori. You closed the door."

"But you can't prove it. I guess it's logical that I opened the root cellar door, but even that can't be proven."

"Why did you do it, man?" asked Nick. "You should have come forward and given the murderer up to the cops. Now you're in trouble. You're her partner in crime."

"Accessory, Nick. He's an accessory," said Lori.

Nick frowned and looked at her for the first time that afternoon.

"Because I, unlike the rest of you rubes, have a cause greater than myself. I have this museum to nurture, to care for, to help grow."

"It's just a museum, you idiot. Abigail and Aggie were human beings," said Nick. "And you were going to let Lori hang for this thing, weren't you? My God, you even had me believing she'd done it. You've got no conscience at all."

Alex began to sort of like the guy again.

Everyone's eyes were on Adrian in case he tried to make a break for it like the others, but the museum director sat back in his chair and sipped his coffee. His face was drawn, but thoughtful. "I don't think any of you get it. Maybe Tasha has an inkling. You don't know how important this place is. Without the past, the present becomes empty, thin, one dimensional. Without the museum, your lives are just Shrubsbury. If the past is a big black hole, then it's not only this place that's nothing. The whole present dissolves. Every object in this museum tells a story of people whose lives would otherwise be lost. Someday it will be your life that will be blotted out—the car you drive, the field you cultivate, your favorite shirt and your brand of coffee. The people you loved and who loved you, or for that matter, the people you hated and who hated you.

"Without people like me protecting the past, holding it sacred, keeping it for the generations, the world would be a sorrier place.

"I know most of you don't understand it, but the museum is in an ongoing struggle to survive, really just hanging on. Aggie knew that but, out of spite for me, she didn't care. She owed this place for so much of the color in her own life, and yet, when she couldn't control it she turned on it. She was willing to see us go down. I hated her for that much more than I hated her for every personal insult I've endured."

Ms. Mulholland looked at him sadly. "All that mental meandering has fogged your conscience, Adrian. You've filled your present with the past until it's overflowing and there's no room for the live human beings you have to live and work with. I knew you had a problem, but I always admired your zeal. Really. You would have let Lori take the blame for the murder."

"You bastard," said Nick. "Do you realize how hard her life is because of the past you so revere? Mine too, for that matter." Nick slipped out of his chair and pulled another chair up next to Lori. He took her hand. She looked at him skeptically.

"I know you're not going to tell us whether you encouraged Abigail to kill Aggie, or stood by and let her do it, which is just as bad, but you do realize that you're about to lose your museum, don't you?" Ms. M said quietly. "You're probably going to prison."

Adrian shrugged his shoulders. "Yes, I know I'll go to prison. And I'm not at all happy about it. I'm going to make a lousy prisoner. But everything I did was for a higher cause. About that, I'm all right. Although I know you don't understand it, I face prison with a clear conscience. It was a good scheme. They were all good schemes. I knew I could blackmail Abigail Shelton for years to come and fatten up the museum's endowment by millions. Abigail wanted to kill the old lady who laughed in her face when she told her, proved to her, that she was her daughter. She'd been looking for her real mother for years. That Aggie had no family feeling, despite her reverence for her own genealogy, is evident; I don't think she ever loved anyone but Nick's father, and then only because she couldn't have him. When Nick came along, the poor cow was besotted with lust for the son of her old lover. There's only one thing you can give her credit for: Aggie never pretended to love people. She did pretend to care about history, the bitch.

"When Aggie died, it looked like everyone would get their just desserts, and the museum would be benefitted besides. I would have taken care of Lori, she wouldn't have gone to jail. It would have been all to the good."

Alex had heard enough. Usually he wouldn't have spoken up in a room of adults—they were all too much like teachers—but he did now. "You know, Mr. Dabney, I always thought you were a silly man, and I still do. Now I see that you're evil too. I never knew before that silly could be evil."

XXXIII

Postlude

It was late October and the leaves were mostly off the trees. The world had turned almost Gothic with hoary trees fingering the passing winds with their bony branches, and the hills all mauve, except for the sudden gold of tamaracks. Ms. Mulholland was taking longer walks. She'd found a sheep dog puppy and decided to raise him, even though her apartment was already cramped. Both she and Gusty—that was the dog's name—needed to get out and move around, and the days were perfect for it. In winter, she'd cross-country ski with him. In the spring they might even run together. They'd certainly play some frisbee.

She hadn't seen much of Alex since the murders were solved, mostly because his mother heard about his escapades and decided she'd rather have a son who was whole and healthy than one who was awesome. At least, that's how Alex put it to her one day when he got off the school bus early and came for cocoa. Ms. Mulholland had become a dangerous influence. She hoped

261

Donna Churchill would forgive her by next summer when it was time for Alex to come back to work, but there was no guarantee of it. She missed him.

Fall had always been a quiet time at the museum. The crafts classes met—the spinners spun, the quilters quilted and the herbalists decanted wonderful potions—but there were no visitors to the Old Shrubsbury School House Museum. It was always a lonely building, even when it was full of people. In the autumn it seemed especially isolated, sad somehow in its rootedness in things that were no more. Even at Christmas, it would remain locked up, while everyone sleighed and sledded around it and drank hot cider in the gift shop across the road. Despite its solitude, though, it was still the focal point of the town of Shrubsbury, the hub around which everything else turned.

Lori had hardly been sprung from jail when she was elevated to the post of temporary director for the museum. She still seemed a little dazed, but with the assistance of the capable Nick Crafts, she was doing fine. The newspapers were less interested in the murder since a flatlander with no real connection to the museum had been indicted.

Adrian was fighting charges and it was very possible that he'd never face trial since there was so little evidence of anything illegal. Even if he got off he'd have to find another museum. The board had publicly dismissed him, although they'd sent him away with a printed flowery edged thank-you for his work for the Old Shrubsbury House Museum.

Tasha hadn't kept up with Major Shelton and Principal Plumbwell. Connecticut seemed so far away, and she found it difficult to care much about either of them. Abigail Shelton was in jail in Newport awaiting trial.

Sera moved into the Hamilton House, cleaned it up and set up a pottery studio in her mother's old bedroom. She still couldn't be sure the house was hers, but she and Ms. M drank tea together there once a week and exchanged horoscopes.

As she took a turn on the road back toward the museum, Tasha caught sight of Alex pedaling towards her. Gusty barked happily and gamboled towards him. Bicycles were her favorite toy of the moment. Ms. Mulholland thanked God that she didn't prefer deer, or worse, porcupines.

"Hey there, Alex," she said, as she caught hold of Gusty's collar and shushed her.

"Hey, Ms. M. Hey, Gusty." He rolled up and fell in beside her, walking his bike. "How are things?"

"Fine. A little slow with no murder, no thievery, not even a misdemeanor graffiti. How's your soccer game? It'll be snowing soon."

"I'm better, Ms. M. Now that I'm cool, I'm better."

"Has it really made a difference? Do you feel different? Do you feel like you're cool?"

"Sometimes," he said. "Not all the time."

"Well, you look different. You must have grown an inch in the last month. Your hair isn't quite as red, and your eyes are bluer.

I'd say you definitely look like a cool guy."

"Ah, Ms. M. How would you know?"

"Even an old gal can tell cool."

He laughed. "We were really good together, weren't we?"

"I'd say so."

"Promise me if there's another murder, we'll solve it?"

"Absolutely."

They walked along, their feet shuffling through leaves, the leaves crackling under Alex's bike tires. Gusty ran from one side of the road to the other, sniffing out mysteries they would never comprehend. Two ravens circled in the sky, crying out to each other.

"I have something for you if you'd like to come up for some cocoa and cookies."

"Yeah, I'd like that."

"But would your mom approve?"

"Probably not. But she forgot to say it this morning for the first time in thirty days. What kind of cookies?"

"Fig newtons. I haven't been baking as much since there's no one to eat them with me."

Alex took the stairs two steps at a time with Gusty right behind him and Ms. Mulholland after that. Inside they heard Winky jumping for safety to the top of the bookcase. Tasha had stopped locking the door again, and Alex pushed through it, looking around, delighted to be back in one of the best spaces he knew. He threw his jacket on the couch and took his favorite chair. "Come on, Winky. Come on, poor cat."

"Ms. M," he said, after he brushed the cat and played with the dog, while he nibbled on a fig newton and watched her making the cocoa, "I think I must be growing up."

"Oh, I hope not. Not yet. Are you in love, Alex?"

"Nah. Nothing like that. Girls are weird, if you know what I mean."

"Hmmmmm."

"You know one of the things I miss most about coming here?"

"What's that?"

"Your cello music."

"Why that's wonderful. That's really wonderful," murmured Tasha Mulholland.

"My mom's going to get me piano lessons. I mean, it'll be groovy piano, of course, but someday maybe I can play with you."

"I'd really like that, Alex." She poured out two cups of cocoa and, as usual, gave him the big purple cup and herself the smaller red one. Then she went to her desk and pulled out the secret drawer. "I thought you should have this since it belonged to your ancestor, Nate Howe. I think he'd have liked you to have Isabelle's locket."

Alex cupped the locket in his hand and gazed at it, smiling happily. "It's my first antique, Ms. M. Thank you."

Before he rode home, Alex stayed for a whole movement of cello music. It wasn't Bach, it was something groovier than that. It was like Ms. Mulholland was meeting him halfway on this music thing.